I0690821

The Book of Queer Saints

Volume I

Edited by Mae Murray
Foreword by Sam Richard

Edited by Mae Murray.

Cover art by Ludo, with edits by Caitlin Marceau.

Cover design by Jordan Shiveley.

Interior formatting and design by Sam Richard and Mae Murray.

Paperback ISBN: 979-8-9893591-0-3

First Edition published March 2022 as *The Book of Queer Saints.*

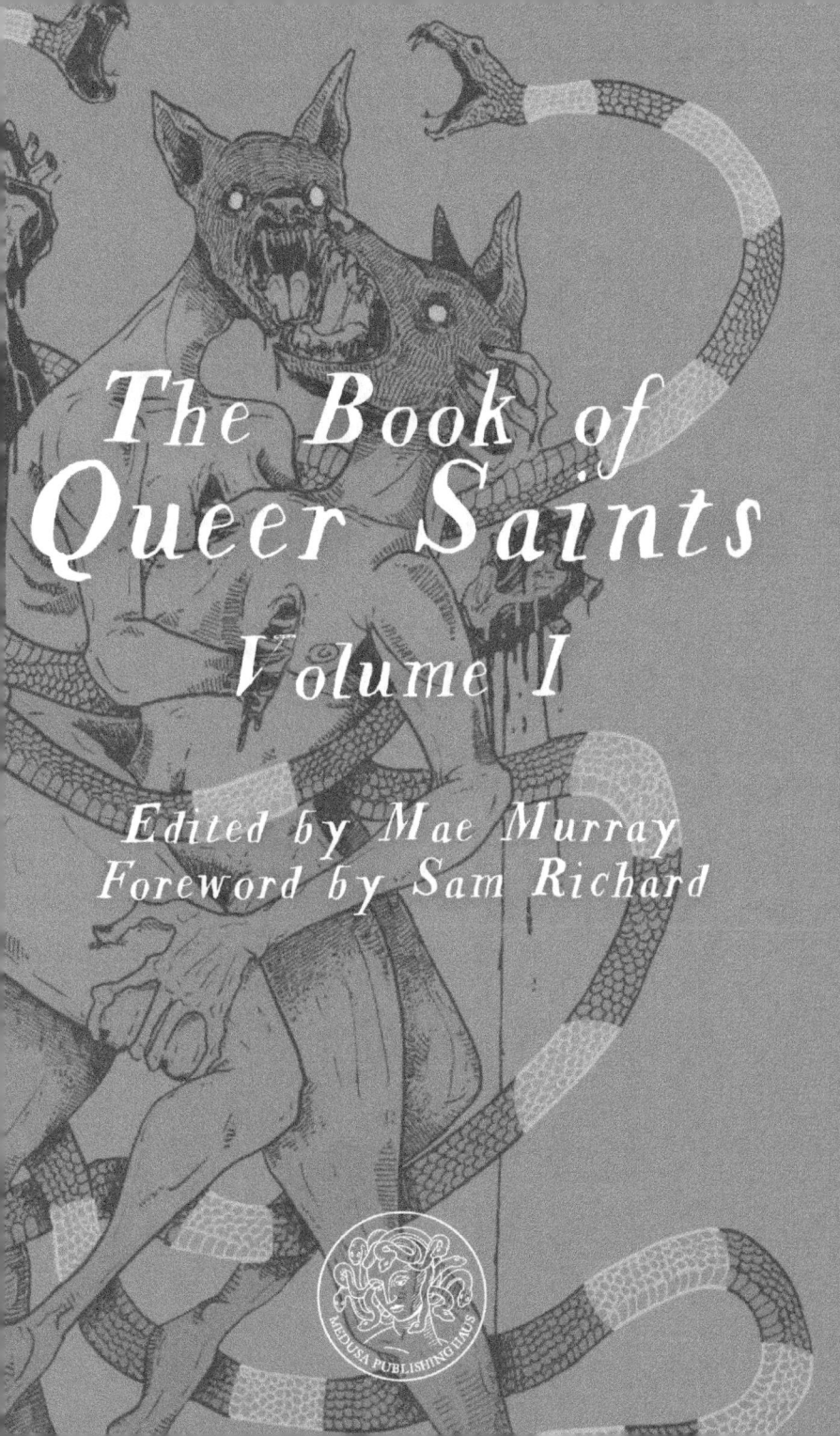

The Book of
Queer Saints

Volume I

Edited by Mae Murray
Foreword by Sam Richard

MEDUSA PUBLISHING HAUS

CONTENTS

FOREWORD

SAM RICHARD

Many months ago, Mae, Eric Raglin, and I had a long conversation about the criticism queer writers have gotten (often by other queer folks) for writing queer characters that aren't socially acceptable and/or 100% morally good. It's an argument that seems to come up over and over again when a book by a queer creator dives into the ugliness of humanity.

I understand the desire to see ourselves portrayed as something more than the queer-coded villain or the overtly queer—but confused—psychopath. And understanding the history of cis-straight men writing or directing or portraying who we are as something 'other' is absolutely something we should all be aware of. However, leveraging that same criticism towards queer creators for being open and honest about their struggles, their fears, their pain— hell, even just their creativity—is a net negative for the community as a whole, for art as a whole.

And this isn't even touching the history of queer literature and just how many important (and even unknown) queer writers have spent time in the murk of putting shitty people doing shitty things into their work.

Queer writers don't owe you squeaky clean queer characters or stories. They don't owe you the type of representation that we're routinely told is important and revolutionary when it comes to major multimedia corporations inserting a two-second-long chaste kiss between queer characters, then never addressing it again; as if that's *meaningful* representation.

If that's the only queer representation we're allowed, then we're doomed.

The writers in this book are a solution to that doom. This is a book full of queer representation that is messy and ugly and uncomfortable and painful. It's a book full of queer characters who are cruel and conflicted and complex and interesting. Yes, queer joy, but also: queer rage, queer hostility, queer panic, queer madness, queer violence, queer horror.

We, much like the characters and stories we write, are capable of more in our art than Chaste Queer Characters Have a Good Day. And that's a fucking good thing. That should be seen as a good thing. And if you don't think it is, then maybe you should check in and ask yourself why you demand artistic purity from queer artists.

The Saints in this book are more than the villainous, amoral, monstrous, outlaw queer characters. The true Saints in *The Book of Queer Saints* are Hailey Piper, Eric LaRocca, James Bennett, Perry Ruhland, Nikki R. Leigh, Joe Koch, Joshua R. Pangborn, K.S. Walker, George Daniel Lea, LC von Hessen, Briar Ripley Page, Eric Raglin, Belle Tolls, and—most of all, for making this whole thing happen—Mae Murray. The true Saints are all the queer writers, artists, and creators who are making art on their own terms.

Sam Richard
March 2022

INTRODUCTION

MAE MURRAY

When I set out to publish *The Book of Queer Saints: Volume I* in 2022, I had no idea what I was doing. I'd never produced a book before, from conception to birth, or nurtured it through its first 18 months. I didn't know what it would become for readers and writers alike, and the passionate following the anthology would gain. I certainly didn't anticipate that it would be nominated for a British Fantasy Award, or that James Bennett's story "Morta" would win the BFA for short fiction.

As I sit here and reflect in the quiet of my office, which is littered with stickers and packing materials and boxes in anticipation for the release of *Volume II*, I can't help but feel overwhelmed with gratitude. I am just one person, doing this alone from a small apartment, but I am not alone in vision.

Queer Saints cracked my world open, allowed me to make connections with other publishers, editors, reviewers, writers, and readers who noticed a disparity in the way queer horror writers were treated as queer representation in literature expanded. Not only that—they supported my mission to publish as many new writers as possible.

I was able to open my micro press, Medusa Publishing

Haus, because of the overwhelming support I've received, and as a result, I've been able to start the Equilibrium Publishing Initiative, an annual pledge for publishers and readers to support the first publication of at least one new writer a year.

This new edition of *The Book of Queer Saints*, now called *The Book of Queer Saints: Volume I*, is a statement on how far this book has come, how far I have come, and how far the writers who were a part of it have come in just 18 months. It is now the first volume of a series. Instead of being published under my name, it is being published under the name of my own publishing company. Some of the writers have won or been nominated for awards as a result of this book. Many have gone on to publish other vital works in the queer horror canon.

I am endlessly proud of this book, endlessly grateful to everyone who has been a part of it and to those who will discover it as it finds new life.

Mae Murray
October 2023

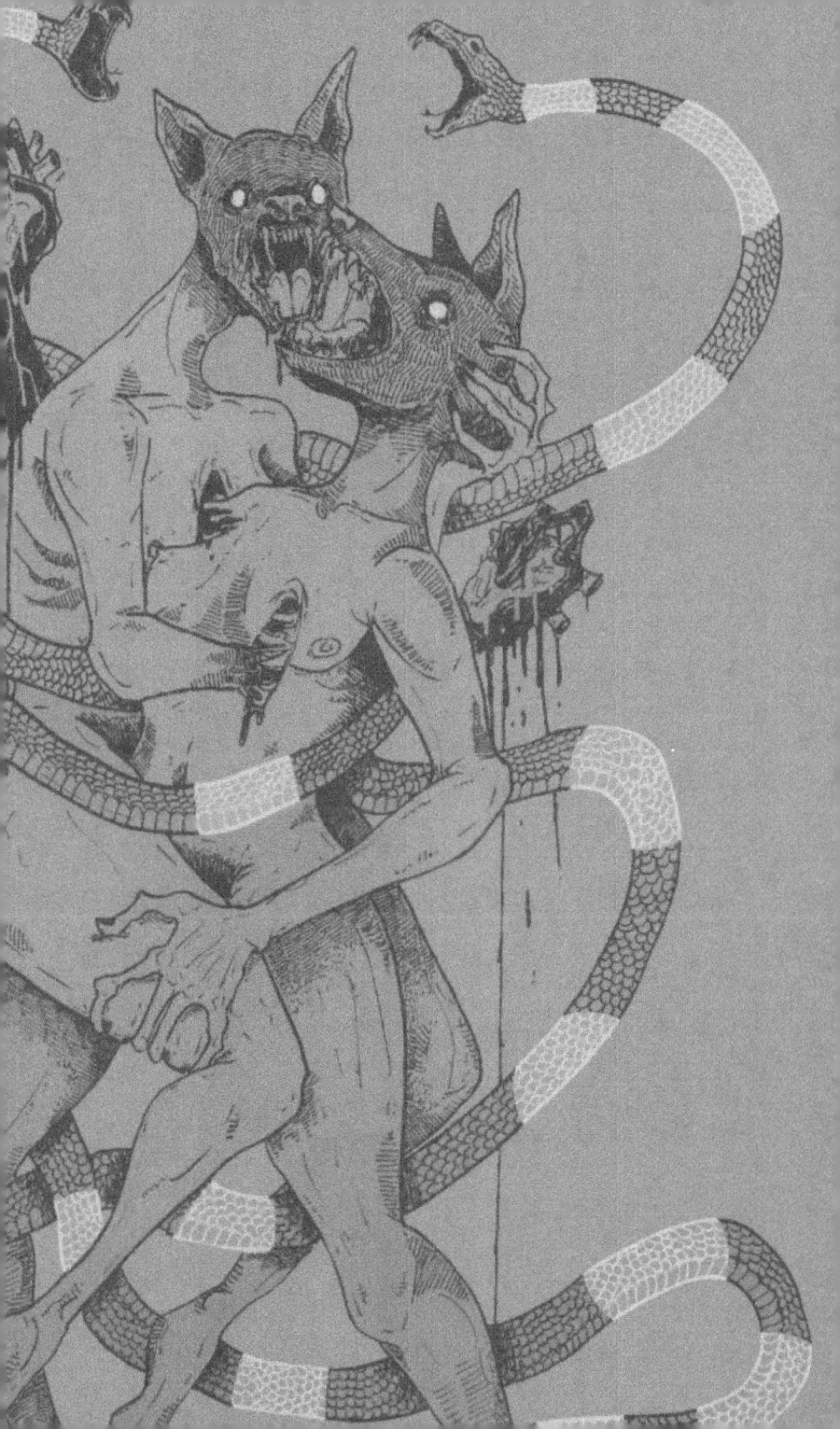

WE FROLIC WITHIN THE LEVIATHAN'S HEART

HAILEY PIPER

A barnacle-scaled boardwalk has seen the last of an orange sunset as starlit Mother Mayoude rises from the depths and releases us into Frolic Night.

If the land-folk were to see, most wouldn't believe, but she makes sure they won't see. Her whale-wide mouth opens in a dark corner of the bay, beside filth-ridden sand and filthier piping, and out we spill from the fleshy pockets in her gums and cheeks and between her me-sized teeth. On most nights, we grab at sea life, caught in her mouth instead of sinking down her throat. Bits of shark, of bitty fish, of crab and seal and squid. Bits of everything.

But tonight we kick across the waves and crawl up the beach, first gasping and then rising on webbed feet. We stretch scaly limbs and flare the great spiny fins along our scalps and backs in displays of crimson and opaque and colors with names I've forgotten.

Shore leave, one sailor called it when Nizi tried to tell him what we are, how our lives work between sea and land. But when he explained his meaning, before Nizi took him into her and then stole his clothes to wear another Frolic

Night, his shore leave seemed a fish of another breed. Sailors work at sea upon their ships, never in the pocketed embrace of a mother's mouth, and then play and rest on the land.

Our Frolic Night isn't the same. Yes, we play—Mother Mayoude wants us to have fun—but our joy is not the night's purpose.

It is a tithing.

When we Children of Mayoude have finished adjusting to the lightness of moist wind and the heaviness of dry land, we climb the sands toward the boardwalk and scatter into scant shadows. These coastal edges used to be dim places but for a tavern here, a lighthouse there. Dark and quiet corners remain across the oceans, but Mother Mayoude can't bring us to them often. The numbers of land-folk in such places shrink between visits, and they often have little joy and fewer treasures worth taking.

If we're going to frolic, we have to brave these bright places of neon swirling circles and flashing bulbs above carnival-like games, where land-folk decorate their necks and limbs in glowing tubes as if luring some smaller prey.

I watch Nizi crouch behind a shed of warped wood, open a plastic bag she found between giant teeth one day, and don her sailor's suit. She's a funny creature in this tattered white-and-blue outfit, but she says that's the point. She'll frolic, and the land-folk will be drawn to her visual strangeness.

Why would a tiny land-folk woman wear a big sailor suit if not for attention? Nizi said to me once. They'll give it, and I'll take more.

I wear loose pants and a hoodie. I don't want attention.

"Cute outfit," a land-folk woman says, baubles shining from her ears, as she passes Nizi. The brick-like land-folk man beside her is watching, they're both watching, and maybe Nizi can take from each of them in her frolicking tonight. I've seen it before.

We Children of Mayoude never frolic together. We'll eye each other from across shadows and lights, but to group together on land is dangerous. Some of us our stolen clothes have tattered and torn apart in Mother Mayoude's jaws to the point it can't hide our scales and fins. Some of us can't pass for land-folk as easily as others, even when clothed. Poor Pomo must stick to dark places, where she nabs balloons and candies, never anything plucked from land-folk bodies. Sometimes she lies in the surf pretending she's a dead animal until unsuspecting land-folk wander close.

In the quiet corners of the world, the land-folk tell stories of us thanks to Children of Mayoude like Pomo. Their elders whisper myths and keep harpoons and firearms ready in case they ever see creatures like her again.

It isn't right. She's no different than the rest of us, but the land-folk treat her so. She can't help her tremendous gills, or that her scales have crossed her facial features. Even if she borrowed my stolen hoodie, the land-folk would never see her as one of them.

The transformation takes each of us in different ways.

I used to wander this boardwalk more often when I had hair instead of scales. The hoodie I wore then was mine and kept me warm against the brisk sea breeze. Nowadays, I keep someone else's hoodie, stolen another Frolic Night, to hide my scalp fin and limb scales.

By then, I had already learned Frolic Night was not a gift but a tithing. We learn this early. There's no confusion when Mother Mayoude demands we go forth and steal.

Music booms from speakers atop narrow wooden poles, these new songs a mystery to me. Land-folk children run by, laughing, their mother chasing them, and I wish to tell her how much easier it might be if she could grow large and carry children in her mouth. When she isn't looking, I pluck the wallet from her open purse, swipe the cash, and drop the leather. Distraught land-folk tend to be distracted, and she doesn't need money like I do. She'll have every night to frolic, but I only have now.

I spot Nizi again outside a trinket shop, wearing mean-looking sunglasses that feel wrong against her pleasant sailor suit. Likely she's stuffed other pairs of them inside her clothes the way she's stuffed herself between the couple who passed her earlier. They each have a hand to the small of her back, and I wonder what she'll take from them.

Our relationship with the land-folk wasn't always resentful and thieving. Mother Mayoude was never young, but when she was another kind of old and the land-folk were fresh creatures on this Earth, they would bring offerings to beaches and coastal crags and clifftops overlooking the sea. The great wet pit of Mayoude would open beneath them, and they would give all she demanded and more. In return, she would let them sail and fish, and she wouldn't harm them.

This was before the land-folk's angry machines and poison. The offerings vanished as they betrayed Mother Mayoude and turned instead to a great taking with no concern for repaying the last of the sea's deep souls.

But Mother Mayoude found a way to make them pay, in bits and pieces.

I tear my eyes from Nizi and her couple before she notices I'm staring. We're not supposed to cluster. When I spot Pomo behind a food truck, I hurry the opposite way down the boardwalk, my loose pants swishing, my webbed feet hidden beneath their wide bottoms. Down the lit walk-ways, past the screams and rides, I search for another open purse, another treasure.

A wooden outcropping juts balcony-like from the board-walk toward the sea, where two women snap at each other along its thin railing. One is stocky and wears silver in her ears, nose, and lips. The other is taller than me, and her hair juts from her head like my scalp fin when flared.

4

Words cut through the air and heels grind into wood. The silver-faced woman reels back one arm, chucks a glass bottle toward the sea, and then storms away. The one with fin-like hair doesn't watch the other go, only glares at the sky as if expectant, chest heaving, teeth bared at the stars.

I wander her way. Distraught land-folk tend to be distracted.

But as I'm about to curl around her side and pick her pocket, she turns to me. A pain writhes in her red-rimmed eyes, but also some species of relief, like she's been waiting for right now to happen for minutes, months, years.

"You lonely?" she asks.

Does she mean I have no one at all, or that I'm alone now? I nod as if answering anything.

"Me too," the land-folk woman says. "I'm Rachel."

My throat muscles battle until they remember her speech. "Quay," I say.

Rachel chins down the boardwalk. "Want to play some games?"

We stroll the boardwalk back the way I came, toward the game stalls that echo seaside carnivals of yesteryear. I've played these before—tossing horseshoes, slamming hammers onto weighing scales, firing squirt guns into clown mouths that could only dream to become the damp dark pit of Mother Mayoude when she surfaces to collect us. If Nizi, Pomo, or any of the others wander near, I don't see them. My attention's caught elsewhere.

Rachel stops us at a stall where a teenager in oversized jacket and undersized tank top explains the rules of chucking darts at balloons. Different balloons give different points, and higher scores mean bigger prizes. Rachel pays for each of us to play, but my hands are clammy and clumsy. I hit one low-value balloon, nothing else, and then watch Rachel lean a dart past her face, back toward her ear, forward again, echoing the harpoon-wielding men upon whaling vessels of

5

yesteryear when they would mistake Mother Mayoude for their prey. Those boats vanished into land-folk legend, their remains never found.

"I wonder about porpoises," Rachel says, never blinking from the balloon-coated wall.

Porpoises. Like dolphins but different. I try to remember if Mother Mayoude has eaten of them; she swallows so much of the sea that she must have. If I'd seen a porpoise, it would only be shrapnel found between motherly teeth.

Rachel chucks her dart. It strikes between two orange mid-value balloons. "I need to ask, Quay—what's your porpoise in life?"

The Children of Mayoude own nothing but ourselves and what we steal from land-folk. I can't own a piece of the sea. That belongs to Mother Mayoude.

"Don't have a porpoise?" Rachel asks, drawing up another dart. "No raisin for your existence? No fate to your bean?"

She giggles so hard, she drops the dart onto the board-walk. Its needle pierces wood, and the gentle land-folk teenager who hands out darts says that should count as a throw, but Rachel's welcome to try again anyway. They're trying to catch her attention, oblivious to her distraction. She doesn't notice them, doesn't even notice me, really. This is mimicry of joy while she glances over her shoulder again and again, as if expecting someone like the silver-faced woman to watch us and react.

I bend to fetch the dart—our frolicking is far from done —but Rachel bends for it too. Our faces hover close in the shadow of the game stall counter. My eyes must be black pits here; I see her perfectly, the hazy uncertainty in her eyes, drunk not with alcohol but with pain. Someone's hurt her worse than she knows how to say.

"Have you ever felt like you're the only real person in the world?" she asks.

Only land-folk could ever see life that way. If a feeling like Rachel's once came to me in the past, I've forgotten it in the mouth of Mother Mayoude.

Rachel's hand cups my jaw, where I hide tiny sharp teeth behind full lips. "No, you wouldn't. You're too full of realness yourself. Only fake people project their bullshit onto everyone else." She plucks the dart from the warped wood beneath us, clambers up the game counter, and throws wild.

The needle pops a high-value balloon. She misses with her final dart, but there's a fire in her now, burning for prizes, for frolic and tithing from the innocent land-folk teen who tends this game stall. Her hands rummage at her jeans, hook fingers into pockets, but nothing pops out except a plastic card emblazoned with her face. She tucks it away and sets fuming hands onto the counter.

I dig into my hoodie's pocket and hand over the money I swiped from the distracted mother before I met Rachel. She stares into me so intensely, for a moment I think she sees the scalp fin tucked beneath my hood.

But then she slides the dollars across the counter and gathers another trio of darts. A low-value balloon bursts beneath the first needle. A high-value one pops beneath the second. The third dart slashes into the wall, but Rachel's already gathering another trio for another try. She doesn't want consolation prizes; she wants something big. Her stare burns the balloons' souls near to bursting before her darts cut past the game counter and into the far wall.

Fury turns to joy when she bursts three big-prize balloons. She hugs an arm around my waist and draws her face close to mine as if we're under the counter again.

As if she wants our faces to touch.

I've seen Nizi with land-folk partners aplenty. Della, Nile, others, even Pomo once, though I doubt that man understood what he was looking at.

Never me. The sailors have been easiest for Children of Mayoude to meet in the past, fueled with drink and frustration, but none ever held my interest, either at sea or during their shore leave. I tried to care, but they were only walking opportunities to steal medallions, keepsakes, precious papers. No intimacy there.

Rachel glows against boardwalk neon, a rhythm to her movements capturing some magic in the alien songs blasting through the air. Her grasp is firm, and I let her bounce us up and down in victory while the young land-folk behind the counter fetches her chosen prize.

We drag away a stuffed white tiger shaped like a teddy bear, its torso larger than my head. It's a treasure I might steal away to Mother Mayoude, but I'm not thinking too hard about tithing right now. I'm thinking about frolicking.

I'm thinking how Rachel's fingers keep worming between mine. A blood-deep pain lurks beneath her skin, and she wants more than anything for someone to root it out. Her eyes seem lost in the night. She doesn't live in purposeful cycles, but a chaotic miasma of existence, always waiting for meaning to drop into her life. I don't know what that silver-faced land-folk woman means to her, but she brought as much confusion and suffering into Rachel's life as she brought joy. Maybe more.

We're another half-dozen game stalls from the darts and balloons, poor in money but rich in stuffed tiger, when a song I recognize finally bursts from the high speakers. The singer has slipped my mind, but I remember the electronic noises and keyboard strokes.

Rachel seems to know this song, too—she tucks our stuffed tiger under one armpit, holds my hands in hers, and pretends to sing. More she mumbles parts of the song and then belts out the chorus in loud, broken squawking. Her noises set a confused tremble in my bones. I shouldn't enjoy this; her singing mimics an unfortunate wading seagull before it drowns in Mother Mayoude's gulping maw.

But I do like Rachel's horrible song. Maybe because I like her and the way she clutches my hands without noticing the faint blue scales along the knuckles. Or she notices and doesn't care, and in that case, I like her even more.

She leads me stumbling between untended game stalls, past boardwalk wood and onto behind-building sand. The shadows hide us from neon, while the air's full of strange new songs, land-folk commotion, and the hush and gasp of the ocean against the nearby shore. There's something perfect about it—if I've ever known the words, I've forgotten them now.

The stuffed tiger drops to Rachel's feet, and my back sinks into the wooden wall behind the derelict game stall as she presses full-bodied into me.

Her kiss is warm and full. I let her take over, the touching old to her but new to me. Does she notice my shrunken ears, or the dark breadth of my eyes on this gloomy side of the boardwalk, or my pointed teeth as her tongue scrapes in and out? I don't think so, at least until her blood-deep pain brings her head creeping up my hoodie's underside, bulging beneath cloth, where she kisses my soft belly and scales.

I could stop her.

Or I could let her discover I'm not like her.

She pauses partway up my chest and then draws her head down and out. Her hands keep my hoodie rolled almost to my neck as she studies my chest, where scales brace nipples and gut, their stripes something like our stuffed tiger, only bluer and greener.

One hand reaches past my face and shoves my hood down. The sensation sends my scalp fin cresting like her hair. One fingertip traces its spines, and a pleasant heat crackles through my bones.

Nizi never mentions how land-folk react when they

discover what she is. From how she tells her stories, in whispers across the inner mouth of Mother Mayoude, the sailors never notice. They feel the same as they would with any land-folk woman, perhaps better, and she plunders their belongings while they sleep afterward.

Rachel notices me. She should be scared, what with the myths land-folk tell of us, but her face is fearless. The pain in her eyes ebbs on a drifting tide into something grander—first realization, and then maybe awe.

And then we're kissing again.

I've never frolicked like this before, even when I walked the land freely like Rachel, with land-folk parents who gave me a land-folk name. I was a lonely cold creature who wandered the boardwalk and sang along to its boardwalk songs, even at four in the morning after the towering speakers went silent and everyone had gone home except the drunks and junkies and me.

That's when I first found Pomo in the sands below, crying tearlessly at empty hands. She had no treasures to bring Mother Mayoude, I later learned.

No more loneliness for me then, and no more loneliness now. No more cold. Rachel is a furnace on two legs, from the molten core at her chest to the fiery crackle of two fingers as they slide between scaly legs and slip inside me. We go on kissing, too, and rubbing, and the fire spreads up my center until I scream inside her mouth. When she slides out of me, I draw down her front, open her jeans, and bury my face into her in the same place her fingers touched me. She sounds pleased, so I stay buried. My gills suck greedily at the air, unsuited for it but trying their best, confused at why there's no water, or why I don't free my lungs to do their work.

I can't explain to parts of my body that this is where I belong, frolicking as I please.

When I finally draw back, Rachel crumples onto me, and we curl against the carnival shed, panting into each other and coiling. She never asks a question about what I am, so I never have to give an answer. We're past any talk of a porpoise in life.

The night slinks by as we doze and wake. I search her fingers for that blood-deep pain and crackling fire, but she's cooler now. Land-folk aren't grown to stay out all night, even on Frolic Night. I cup my hands around her fingers to warm them, and then we rise together and stroll from the board-walk to the beach, hand clasping hand. Sand crunches under-foot, dry and then damp where lingering waves beat at the shore. Rachel looks to the starry sky like before, but not in the same way. A crucial organ has turned inside her, once twisted upside-down, now set right.

I hope I did that.

As the surf abandons the sand in crescents of white foam, a black swell bulges beneath the waves like a head beneath a hoodie, and the water tears open around a great dark maw.

Rachel glances at pounding footsteps around us as the other Children of Mayoude come rushing from boardwalk to shore. Nizi carries sparkling necklaces and a pair of gold-plated watches, and she stuffs them into her bag with her sailor suit. Pomo carries an armload of pilfered fried meats, some yet steaming in the red dawn. The rest of our kind throw off stolen garments, gather treasures, and carry them into the surf to head home. We like our land treasures, and it is enough for Mother Mayoude we've taken from the land-folk, even if she can't use what we've stolen.

"Is that where you come from?" Rachel asks, chinning toward the sea. "Is that where you're going?"

I nod, and I nod again. These are neither truths nor lies, only incomplete sides. My hand squeezes Rachel's finger.

She stares into my eyes, still awed, but the pain is back, too. "Guess this is goodbye."

She slides her hand from mine, cups my face between her palms, and kisses me again, deep and wet as the sea. Her tongue flicks over mine and rubs purposefully against the sharp points of my teeth, as if she wants them to nick her flesh and fill our mouths with her blood and its pain. I latch my arms around her back, pushing into the kiss.

And then I pull at her body, deciding this is not goodbye.

Rachel fights her mouth from mine and kicks at the sand. "Quay!" she cries.

But my legs are used to kicking, the muscles stronger than hers. I launch us backward from the shore, headed for the horizon where dark waves meet the red-tinted sky. The lowering tide helps me carry Rachel toward the gaping maw at sea, same as it helped Pomo drag me toward Mother Mayoude years and years ago. I jerked and slapped and scratched land-folk fingernails at sea-weathered scales the whole journey, the same as Rachel. My fighting didn't matter then, and Rachel's fighting doesn't matter now. We're already too far from shore for her to swim and escape the coastal shelf's riptide. Even if she slithered out of my grasp, Mother Mayoude's submergence would suck at the ocean surface and drag Rachel drowning into the deep. No one would hear her last scream.

Better she follow me into the motherly abyss, where she'll grow scales and fins and become one of us Children of Mayoude.

I look to her through the watery swirl and rush. Her hands have quit beating, her legs quit kicking. Now she stares inches from my face, lips pursed tight against saltwater spray, her tired eyes asking me through lurching waves: Why?

Her question will be answered as soon as we flow over the gargantuan oceanic lip and into Mother Mayoude's waiting jaws. Fleshy pockets will embrace us, and while the others count their treasures, I'll know mine is one, greater than a stuffed tiger. A land-folk woman, a Rachel, a one-of-us-to-be as Mother Mayoude's saliva begins its work.

Why? The answer lies upon this tongue, between these teeth, within these gums. Despite what she's given me, and I've given her, Rachel will learn the same as the rest of us that Frolic Night is not a gift. Though we have fun and joy, that is not the night's purpose.

It is a tithing.

THE NEON HOLOCAUST

ERIC LAROCCA

I should despise the house you've built from my bones—the framework you've summoned from my despair, the structure you've forged from my anguish the same way a welder heats and remakes metal. I should loathe the little cruelties you made me suffer for the sake of your comfort, the abuses I was forced to endure simply for the good of your luxury and taste.

"This is how it's supposed to be," you'd tell me when I would question the viciousness, when I would oppose your cruelty. "This is why most people don't love each other their whole lives."

I often wondered how you could be so certain. After all, my parents had been happily married for thirty-seven years. When I would mention this, you'd say how it wasn't a fair comparison because "they weren't faggots like us."

"They weren't monsters the way we were," you would tell me, as if your monstrosities were mine to claim as well.

Of course, others were well accustomed with your vindictiveness, your unforgiving nature and the way in which you drain a person of everything until they're as empty, as uniquely bloodless as centipedes. There were countless before me—wraiths of young men that lingered near us when we were in love. If you could even call it being in love.

I'm sure you didn't.

I've searched my mind for a semblance of hatred to spare for you—an appearance of hostility or even a hint of animosity for the unkind and malicious acts you performed on me—and I seem to go wanting whenever I sense revulsion is near. It's almost as if it were impossible for me to despise the very thing you became once you were finished with me, once you had your way with me and left me to rot the way all predators abandon half-dead carrion.

My stomach curls when I think of how exquisitely divine it feels to find myself in a place as innocuous as the corner where two walls meet. My ribcage—your windows framed with painted white shutters. My shoulders and neck—your stairwell with the alabaster handrail. My mind, the private, most unspoiled places where my thoughts collect like rainwater in a storm drain—your bedroom.

I've been told I would be a far more sympathetic victim if I stayed as small and as quiet as you had willed me to be—if I tried not to provoke you or if I neutered myself the way the world seems to want all feminine gay men to castrate themselves.

It's funny how most people love queer men as long as they're sexless, as long as their genitalia is as smooth and as shiny as a plastic doll's. Heterosexual women are playful and coy, as if somehow their appeal might inspire us as long as we remain indifferent and careless to their advances. The heterosexual men that tolerate us only do so because they've rejected our sexuality. To them, we're as sexually ambiguous as a monastic choir boy.

I often wondered if you might prefer me to resemble that. You already seemed to delight in my androgyny—the lingering glances from older men and women in public, their bewildered stares as if struggling to properly assess my gender: something they could never understand.

I wonder—still do—if you understood.

I should hate you. I should despise the nest you've built from my body—from the others that came before me and that were imprudent enough to place their trust in you.

But I don't.

I'm incapable of loathing you and the atrocities you brought upon me for your sheer amusement.

I can't help but wonder if you hate yourself as you wake to endure another day in your childhood home—the place where you learned to masturbate, the house where you skinned pet rabbits with your father's razor, the home where you learned that to love another man was an unforgivable perversity that earned punishment.

I often wonder if that's why you had kept us here—the ones you had murdered, the ones you had robbed of their anatomy to construct the larger, more ornate parts of your home, the ones you had seduced and then left for dead.

The lover you had met on a trip to Cincinnati—the eternal wellspring of his blood watered your mother's garden and kept her roses in bloom even when they had a mind to wither and die. The gentleman you had met in a BDSM chat room who talked too much so you decided to rip out his tongue—his essence now corkscrews the spiral staircase you had installed last month. The young man you had met and routinely fellated while in college—his veins now spiderweb across your ceiling like dark threads and trickle toward the stonework you've arranged near the home's main fireplace.

"Fags deserve what they get," you would tell me.

When I reminded you of your penchant for the male anatomy, you'd dismiss me and remind me that there was a difference between making love and fucking.

"Making love is what men and women do," you would say. "All we can do is fuck."

But I think the most unsavory, the most reprehensible thing you said to me was your matchless assessment of the AIDS crisis.

"Why don't they just call it what it really was?" you would ask me. *"The Neon Holocaust."*

You'd laugh, amused by your cruelty, your disregard for the suffering of countless queer men who were neglected by the government and allowed to perish before it was their time.

You would tell me how you had visions of mass burial sites—the lifeless bodies of queer men piled high on top of one another in their backless hospital gowns and their skin peppered with dark lesions. You'd imagine the machinery rummaging through the maze of corpses, bodies carelessly tossed aside as if they were never someone's child, someone's dear love, someone's absolution.

"Why do you gleefully think of something so horrible?" I would ask you.

You'd look surprised at my brashness. You had thought your reprimanding and constant chastising had rendered me as toothless as a newborn.

"It's what they deserve," you would tell me. "All faggots should be buried alive. It's the worst thing I can think of."

It certainly wasn't the worst thing you could think of. You saved your more perverted and reprehensible thoughts for the young men you lured into your home. It wasn't until recently that I realized you were creating your own Neon Holocaust—the bright colored clothing of the men you murdered left discarded on the bedroom floor to be tossed in the furnace and burned until they were black ashes. Your Neon Holocaust—the neon-colored mass grave you've confined between your walls, the rainbow casket you've made of your childhood home.

I should tell you it was never my intention to harm you. It was never my objective to make you suffer the way you had made the rest of us suffer before death. If you could even call this death, that is. It could probably be better defined as existing in the imperceptible space between life and death— the dim, clouded film as thin and worn as cheesecloth where spirits may gather.

"What have you done?" you ask us, pacing the room in your bathrobe and occasionally attempting to undo the locks that have been welded in place. "Let me out of here."

One of the youngest men you had killed sprouts from his resting place nestled deep in the bookshelf where you had arranged the broken bits of his bones like sea glass scattered on an empty beach. He's dressed in a paisley shirt and his mouth is secured with a ball gag you had fixed there during one of your more enthusiastic sessions of fucking. He removes the ball gag and speaks to you directly:

"You'll stay with us. Take care of us the way we took care of you."

You stare at him, incredulous.

I wonder if you believe him.

You'd probably dispatch him again if you had the opportunity—if you were furnished with the weapon and the time to hack him into little pieces once more.

It's then I remove myself from where you had planted me —from where you had buried me and kept me as if I were a dangerous exotic plant—and I peel myself away until I'm threadbare and at your feet like a limbless beggar.

"All faggots should be buried alive," I tell you with the same matter-of-factness you had once shared with me. "It's the worst thing I can think of."

I see your eyes widen as you come to understand—the coffin you've built for yourself and for your lovers. Even if you were unwilling to call them your lovers when they were alive, they very much think of you as a lover now. Despite your roughness, despite your antagonism, they've loved you in silence for so long as they've watched you bring others to your home and build them into the sturdy framework you've fashioned for a home in such a desolate part of New England. The cops don't come because they don't care.

After all, who actually cares when a faggot dies?

That's what you've said for so long.

I should despise the house you've built from our bones. I should loathe the place where you've buried me—the darkest corner of the house where I now call home. I should yearn for the moment when the monstrosity you've created catches fire and when the grounds are scattered with salt.

But I don't.

I think that's perhaps why this has happened. Because I've willed it to be, just as you willed us to be your victims. I've ached for your criticism, for your unkindness, for your vindictiveness and cruelty. I've yearned for the moment when I can melt into your embrace, when everything around me dims to a soft hum and I feel utterly whole again.

You seem to recognize the fact that this is your home now —that there's nothing you can do to leave, that this is the coffin you've built for yourself and that your resting place will be shared with the young men you slaughtered.

You surrender, if only for a moment, and as we drown in a tide, in a restless current of bodies, I tell you how much you mean to me and how desperately I yearn to make love—the love we were never allowed to make because you deemed it too objectionable.

"Soon," you tell me.

The parts of me that haven't melted into thought yet are able to smile because I know we've changed you. Even if I haven't changed you fully, I know that the Neon Holocaust is over—the horrible ordeal you've created for the ones you loathed the most. Perhaps you'll love us in your death.

"This is how it's supposed to be," I tell you. "There may be a reason why most people don't love each other for their whole lives, but there's no excuse for it in death."

I know what you're thinking. This is just further proof that faggots like us can't be happily in love and that it takes them dying to find solace in one another's company, almost as if our death were contrition for the parody of our character. That's not true. Our love was always destined to end this way. I was always supposed to be your victim and you were always intended to be mine.

I pull you deeper into the parts of the house only we seem to know about—a distant realm where we shrug off our dewy coats of skin and burrow into the places where we know our sadness cannot follow.

Even if sorrow does find us, we have one another to hold for comfort, and eternity has promised us kindness even if we do not deserve it.

MORTA

JAMES BENNETT

*E*ver since the day I ate Frank, I knew I wasn't like the other boys. This was in Cinder, Idaho, about two years ago. And I didn't exactly *eat* Frank, to be fair. It isn't like it matters now anyway; no one ever found him and no one is going to find him either. At the time of Frank's disappearance, nobody gave me a second glance. I looked like any other teenage boy going through their junior year at the Cinder County High School. And through the long dark tunnel of adolescence, which is why I was sitting on the bleachers that August afternoon after Math, watching the football practice and, more specifically, Tiger Perez.

I sat there, my podgy, pale self with the scruffy hair and spectacles, watching the boy of my dreams. Tiger, the quarterback, moved like his namesake, a rippling, bubble-butted, second-generation Puerto Rican in helmet, shoulder pads and oh-so-tight white pants. Every time he caught the ball, my heart flip-flopped in my chest a little.

Frank Kovalevsky materialised from the fading sunlight to remind me that Tiger Perez didn't know I existed.

"What you mooning over him for?" Frank asked, round faced and sneering. "Is it because he's an *alien* like you?"

23

By the sound of him, Frank thought this was hilarious. It was true Mother had told me we weren't from around here, and the dreams I'd been having supported that. One thing's for sure—wherever we're from, it's a lot farther away than Puerto Rico. It explains my name anyway, Morta, which sounds anything but local to Cinder, Idaho. Or anywhere for that matter.

"My worm. We gave you a strong name. A *Brood* name," Mother told me one night long ago, closing her book at my bedside and leaving me to sink into dreams of purple skies, blasted hills and the high, wild shrieking on the wind. The stories and the past she had given me. "A name for an imago. A herald."

Oh, I was special to Mother. And to Frank, it seemed, the latter for less obvious reasons.

"You look weird," his seventeen-year-old mouth offered out of nowhere. "Your hair is all grey and your eyes are funny. It's no wonder the other kids hate you."

I cringed, expecting further insults or even a fight, right here where Tiger would see us. Under this, a grim thrill that at least it might get his attention.

Instead, in that distant, fateful moment, Frank Kovalevsky offered me his hand.

"But I like you. You're cute. Lemme buy you an ice cream downtown."

I looked up at him and I could see from the fire in his cheeks that he meant it. Half bewildered, half hopeful, I reached out and took the hand in question. I didn't even know what I was doing. Was I betraying Tiger by doing so? Such stupid teenage fears...

By the time we reached the entrance to the stadium, Frank was screaming. A minute ago, he'd been whining that my grip was too tight. Sticky. When he tried to wrench it away, I looked down and saw that his hand was melting into mine – and not in the romantic sense. My crotchets were out, excited by contact, I guess. Shit. I was *secreting* again. It'd been happening more and more that last semester, but nothing like this. As Frank wrestled and yelled, the noise from the football field covering his anguish, I placed my other hand over his mouth. It was all I could do. Frank's hand was a liquefied mess, hanging in pink and red rags. Blisters. Shards of bone. Blood and acid peppering the grass. The substance of him absorbed by my own.

Mother had warned me about this. "You're drawing to the end of your larvae phase," she said. "All grown up now."

Frank wasn't going to stop screaming. If I'd tried to free him once digestion had begun, I'd only do damage to myself. There was nothing else to do but drag him into the shadows of the bleachers and devour him whole.

MOTHER WAS the first to come out here. She was proud of it, often telling me, her captive audience, how she'd lain her eggs under the skin of the world and pushed through the membrane that kept it apart. The effort had seen her emerge in the Craters of the Moon National Preserve on the Snake River Plain, central Idaho, a vast volcanic park a few miles to the north of us. But Mother's arrival had nothing to do with outer space or Jurassic activity. Clutching her surviving egg (hello!), she crawled and fluttered her way into Cinder, twenty-one years ago. Father never made it. Burned up in the translation, she said, though the way her eyes flashed made me wonder whether she maybe hadn't consumed him. Post-natal cannibalism wasn't uncommon among the Brood, I'd learned. If you looked into her eyes, you'd find the same shade of violet as mine. If you *really* looked, you'd notice each one is divided into these tiny hexagons, thousands of ommatidia—compound eyes, Mother calls them—but you wouldn't see any of her secrets.

"Never speak to the Watchers," she warned me last year, gripping my arm over the breakfast table in our darkened kitchen. It was the first day of my senior year and I guess she thought I was old enough. Plus all the fuss over Frank Kovalevsky had since died down. "A missing person," the police chief said on the news with an air of sad finality. Even the posters on the telegraph poles were fading. Fading like Frank in my system...

"Damn scientists. You know they're watching the house, right? Always watching. And they'll only get spunkier the older you get, Morta. Another season and you'll be ready. The Hour of Emergence will come. And then glory, glory, sweet glory," she sang it, buzzing. Then frowned. "It's your purpose, my worm. So watch out!"

This answered why the blinds were always drawn, even in summer in the middle of the day. I mean, it's true we don't like the light much anyway—weren't my spectacles made of a special material to keep out the worst of the rays?—but there was another reason too, a darker one. It was why we only spoke to the neighbours if necessity forced our hand (Oh, we'd gone without cups of sugar just fine). Perhaps it answered why the cars with the smoked glass windows sometimes pulled up on Gannett Lane, their engines rumbling, but never stopping. No one ever getting out.

"Watch the Watchers," I said. I thought I was so smart at the time. "But how will I know if—"

"You'll know." My arm was hurting; Mother didn't stop squeezing when she got her panties in a bunch. "The Exterminators have a smell. All in the cult do. And you don't want one of those fuckers to get their mitts on you, trust me."

"Mom!"

"Hush now. Give thanks to the Nest and eat. You'll be late for class."

With this, Mother shrilled out a brief prayer. She kept it low; it'd burst next door's eardrums if they overheard. Then she regurgitated over the flesh on the table, the raw, bubbling lump that hailed from a source I knew better than to ask about, and that was the end of the conversation.

I went off to school, to my senior year and my last, with Frank Kovalevsky—the essence of him, that is—howling faintly in my mind.

Our prey doesn't die right away, you see. Mother taught me that too. The flesh dissolves, but the spirit lingers, granting energy. Strength.

In a way, Frank didn't die at all.

It's kind of a comfort to hear him in there.

I'M... *evolving.* The fairy tales Mother told me have turned into dreams. The glint of purple skies off a carapace, the flutter of wings and the shrieking on the wind (the swarm song, Mother tells me) often wake me at night in the upstairs bedroom, covered in sweat and a kind of mucus, acidic and white. It isn't noxious to me. It's still pretty gross. *Wet dreams.* I read about them in a book. Nocturnal emissions don't soak you from head to foot though. They don't stink of batteries and rot.

Believe me, I'd much rather dream about Tiger Perez.

I'm nineteen now. A third instar, Mother says, if not quite a man. Frank is a distant echo. I'm the Herald of the Brood. But to Tiger Perez, I may as well be dead.

Tiger never made it to university. Some kind of misunderstanding with a cheerleader, as I understand it, that saw him kicked off the football team. And no team, well, no scholarship. It wasn't like he was acing Math. Tiger got a job pumping gas in downtown Cinder and sure, it sucks balls, but it was good news for me.

It's good news because I'm not going to university either. Mother told me she didn't think it was smart, what with incubation and all. "No one wants to see that in the canteen," she said. "They'll try to stop you, Morta. They'll bring fire and Lord knows what else."

This ominous prophecy faded into insignificance next to the fact that I could spend all afternoon at the Cinder Public Library. The Cinder Public Library has big clean windows and sits on Main, right opposite the station where Tiger pumps gas, checks oil and kicks tyres.

"Always the same book," Mrs. Blum said over the counter one day. I was returning *Changing Bodies: The Easy-As-Pie Puberty Book For Boys* (which hadn't been helpful at all), but it was the *Birdwatching For Beginners* book that she was talking about. "I don't think you're gonna see a woodpecker or a red-tail on the intersection, honey. Might wanna get up to the preserve for that."

I blushed. What the hell did she know? I could tell her things about Craters that would make her squeal and piss herself. Instead, I mumbled something about a roosting owl in the gables of the store over the street. It explained the binoculars hung around my neck. Traffic often got in the way and sometimes Tiger was at the register or in the garage and I couldn't see him. It was worth it for the times I could. He'd lost none of his draw in his dirty overalls, his sin-black hair slicked back under a baseball cap. Sure, I couldn't see his ass as well as I used to in his football pants, but when he leant over a hood to clean it—*phew!* And his sleeves were rolled up to show his forearms, the fuzz of hair and pop of veins on his golden brown skin, suggesting how they might feel wrapped around me, how they might feel against my lips...

"Heck, it's your life. If I was you, I wouldn't wanna spend it in this dump."

With that, Mrs. Blum returned me to the pond of oblivion

and turned to another customer. Grey-haired, bespectacled, half-drowned in my clothes, I shuffled over to the tables by the windows, relieved to find my usual seat empty. I could already see Tiger across the street, grinning his diamond grin at another satisfied customer (why wouldn't they be?) and accepting a dollar bill tip. There was always the fear that he'd look up and see me, a thrill in the pit of my stomach, even though I was far away and stood behind glass, like a bug pinned to a display case.

Today, there was a different thrill. Before I sat down I heard books falling, slapping on linoleum. When I turned in that direction, I saw a man looking at me through a gap in the shelves. His hat was tipped down over his face and for some reason he was wearing shades, even in the gloom of the library.

It was only a split second. Had he pushed the books aside to get a better look at me? Mother told me I'd *smell* it when I saw one, and the prickling of my skin confirmed the fact. As did the faint stink of batteries and rot, a thin sheet of gunk bleeding from my skin. Crotchets, a multitude of tiny barbs, emerged on the palms of my hands and scratched at the cover of *Birdwatching For Beginners*. The book hissed, the slip-on polythene bubbling.

Only a split second. Then the man spun on his heel and *vamoosed*. All he left was an echo of heels as he took off, swallowed by the depths of the library.

A *Watcher*. An Exterminator.

I didn't stay to watch Tiger that day.

MY DREAMS WERE GETTING INTENSE. Even in daylight, the memory of purple lingered. The swarm song was growing louder and so it should, Mother said. "They're waiting, Morta," she told me. "Behind the sky. Waiting for the Emergence." In my mind, the shattered plain of Craters didn't compare to the landscape I wandered in sleep.

Perhaps the dreams were why I kept seeing the cars, their smoked glass windows rolled up, their engines running in the neighbourhood. Twice, I saw them downtown. In fact, I was heading downtown when the Watcher appeared, stepping out from an alley between a hair salon and a shutdown bookstore.

"Pardon me, young man. May I have a minute of your time?"

He sounded friendly enough. He looked like all of the others. Dark hat. Dark glasses. Dark suit. And the smell. The smell that was really *my* smell. Sulphur and sewage. Instinct. Alarm.

"Sorry. I'm late," I said, stupidly. Sure, late for the Cinder library and peeper-creeping on Tiger Perez.

"It'll only take a *moment.*"

The word was more of a grunt. The man lunged towards me. Too late, I saw the flash of metal in his hand, heard the jangle of handcuffs ripped from his pocket. On the street, a car pulled up, black as death, its rear door popping open. The Watchers, the cult, meant to abduct me. It didn't take a genius to see that.

"Get offa me!"

I'm no fighter. Usually I prefer to sit in the shadows, happy to be forgotten about. It's safer that way. The attention on me now was like a lamp and despite the man's greeting, unkind. I lashed out, a clumsy swing as he made a grab for me, a handful of sweater in his grip. He stumbled, shimmying towards me, and this time my hand connected—a perfectly aimed slap to the face.

A few things happened at once. One, the man dropped his handcuffs, steel tinkling on the sidewalk. Two, the car pulled off, its door slamming, screeching out onto Main. Thirdly, the Watcher, the member of the Cult of Unseen Stars, started screaming. And why not? My crotchets were hooked in his face. His cheek was already waxen, giving way to runnels of blood, dissolving flesh and tissue. His scream was lower than Frank Kovalevsky's had been. Less shocked, I guess. Later, I put it down to the fact that the man knew exactly who I was, what I was capable of. He knew who Mother was too, according to her. Where she'd come from and what she meant to do. Her son's glorious purpose. Her worm.

The Watcher was screaming and I had to put a stop to that. Traffic on Main wasn't so dense. Thankfully, there were few pedestrians, the town drunk and some old dude. In seconds, however, someone was going to come running. So I clamped my other hand around the man's throat. It was all I could think of to do.

He flailed at me. Blindly, because one of his eyes had gone the way of milkshake, a ball of white bubbles. Relief spread through my guts. The Watcher's cries sank into a gargle. Then silence. He slumped, his head lolling on his chest as his Adam's Apple deliquesced, the mess running over my hand, my sleeve. *Ew.* Teeth clenched with the effort, I dragged the man (I'm pretty strong too. Did I tell you that?) into the alley from which he'd sprung, tossing him down in a clatter of garbage cans, a fan of trash.

I couldn't exactly leave him there. Absorption took a good ten minutes, but at least he wasn't making any noise.

The rats looked on, dumbfounded.

THANK the Nest that I'd wiped my mouth by the time I stepped out of the alleyway. My hair must've looked like Einstein's, a wild grey mop. All the same, the stars smiled down, or maybe they didn't, because Tiger Perez was standing right there on the sidewalk.

"Hey! It's Morta, ain't it?" That's what he said, my flame,

my light, the one I was drawn to like a moth even though it burnt me so. "Morta from school?"

Now it was my turn to melt. I shifted from foot to foot. Stuck a hand in my pocket, my fingers closing with a squelch. My binoculars threatened to pull me into the dirt, as heavy as the One Ring in that movie I'd watched with Mother.

In a voice that came from dimensions away, I said, "Sure."

Tiger was on his way home from work. He worked at the gas station down the street, he said. Roses shone in his cheeks, his eyelashes batting, and he confessed he'd dropped out of school. Like a goon, I nodded along to all of these things, trying to convey the absolute truth that all of it came as news to me.

When he looked at me again, it was furtive. Was I losing my mind?

"That's why you never saw me no more on the football field. Guess it must've taken a while to realise that. Sorry."

"I never... I didn't..."

"It's cool." Tiger took a step towards me. I thought I was going to die, my heart was beating so fast. "I appreciate the support."

"You..." It was like my throat had collapsed. Karma is a bitch. "You play good."

Tiger laughed. "Right."

There was a pause. The street, the library, the world had all gone, swept away in a storm of nerves. Tiger Perez was all there was, grinning at me on the sidewalk.

"I should probably—" Escape. Run. Cut a hole in the sky and scram. Anything.

"Say, are you hungry?" he said. "'Cos I know this great burger joint. It ain't far. Come on, amigo. You can keep me company."

The last thing on my mind was food.

I stood there, my belly full, my skin damp under my clothes. My mind full of screams. Loud ones.

The last thing I was gonna do was say no.

I AM in love with Tiger Perez. Oh, it's dumb, I know. Ever since our date (well, it wasn't *really* a date, but yanno), Cinder, Idaho, has become a different place. Not to bring the schmaltz, but the sound of the wind through the trees almost drowns out the rustling behind the sky, the membrane that keeps this world from beyond. And I've stopped visiting the library. I've stopped because I message Tiger instead and we go to the movies or the park. It's summer and we sit on the grass. Drink Coke. Talk about what a shitshow school was.

Sometimes Tiger starts to talk about football and girls. I always change the subject and he drops it. Guess he can tell I'm not like the other boys. He's lonely, I think. An only child like me. His Papa works over at the Wilson Packing Factory and saved up everything to put Tiger through school, so times aren't *estupendo* for Tiger. His future is far from as glorious as mine.

Still, he's my flame. There's this feeling in my stomach, a new thrill. We sit under the drowning trees and I'm going to make him love me back.

Last Friday, he told me, "You got funny eyes, you know that?"

He tried to take off my glasses, but I wouldn't let him. The last thing I wanted was a migraine.

"Yeah."

That's when he touched my face. Only lightly. And oh-so-brief.

"Don't worry about it," he said. "They're kind of... special."

He was the quarterback of Cinder County High. I guess appearances can be deceiving.

I want to hold his hand, but I can't.

～

AUTUMN. The best time of year. The long evenings were made for me, the shadows stretching over the lawns like arrows to a future I couldn't see. *The Emergence. Glory.* My eyes hurt less in the dwindling noon light. The screams in my mind were dwindling too. With Frank Kovalevsky it'd been a new thing; the Watcher's torment wasn't such a buzz.

Yeah, I was glad to hear him fade, sucked into my system like the leaves into next door's yard vacuum. No bones. No problem. It was like Time had drawn the blinds on the world, not just in the house on Gannett Street. The pervasive smell of rot was everywhere—in the grass, the bark, the wilting flowers—and it felt like a cocoon of comfort, the cause of which was hard to place. Mother said that the earth itself was a fruit. As it ripened, at the peak of its sweetness before the first brown spots of decay, the swarm would muster and come.

At my call.

"But before all that," Mother said, her eyes gleaming in the kitchen. "Comes incubation." It'd been a long hot day and she was tired from the housework and the spinning; she'd peeled back her hairband, her wig and a bunch of borrowed flesh to let her antennae weave free. "Soon, Morta. Soon."

I never told her about the fight with the Watcher. I told myself it was because I didn't want to worry her. The truth was I was scared she'd ground me, her defenses going up like bulletproof wings. If that happened, I wouldn't be able to sneak off to see Tiger anymore. Tiger, at this point, had turned into an exquisite torture, and I was sad, sure. I'm not like him (or any boy), and even if he were to kiss me, I can't guarantee he wouldn't get, well, *stuck*.

There was a sweetness to the sadness too. An ache. It made my balls hum. My cock felt bruised when it swelled against the front of my jeans. It was like every five minutes! I couldn't stop thinking about him on top of me, brown and slick, my hands on his butt like I'd won bags of gold. At night, I'd grit my teeth as I jerked off so Mother wouldn't hear me in the next room. I was dying, I guess. It was a kind of death. The sheets were caked every morning. Acid burned holes in the mattress.

"Adolescence," I said, shrugging at Mother's frown as she once again crouched before the washing machine.

"Metamorphosis," she snapped back.

Embarrassing.

That Thursday afternoon in late September, I wished I'd told Mother about the Watcher. I was coming home from the park when I heard the scream. Too low, too gruff to be hers. The stink of batteries, a sulfuric tang, joined the aroma of dead leaves, the ghost of rain. My crotchets were out and the twin lumps under my hair—a new addition—were throbbing by the time I reached the front door. It stood wide open, and in the middle of the day, an event so rare it sent sparks up my spine. Between that and the cars parked on Gannett Street, hoods askew, engines running, I knew that things were far from peachy.

I crashed down the hall and into the living room, tearing thick strands of silk out of my way. I was only half-surprised to find the Watchers in the house. Three of them, two men and a woman. One of the men had Mother in a headlock. The woman (*agent,* some memory that wasn't my own whispered) was on her knees, the coffee table upended. *Time* magazine lay open, splayed in this place where time was running out. The bitch was trying to cuff Mother's ankles with what looked like a bicycle lock (but wasn't).

The other man was dancing in the doorway with his back to me, an object in his hand that I took for a gun at first, then realised was a Taser. Darts on thin copper wires speared Mother's breast, her belly. She was spasming and hissing, foam on her lips, a distended, impossible leer. Scraps of blouse and appropriated flesh flew this way and that from her struggles. Her wings had unfurled with the volts jolting through her, veined, iridescent and purple. Their span had smashed pictures from the walls, dislodged ornaments and toppled the lampshade. The air in the room was a pall of electricity, gunk and dust.

When her eyes met mine, I heard her voice ring in my head.

Morta!

I was the Herald, but she was my own. To witness her pain was a slap, snapping me out of my daze. Oh, I was *lightning* then. The man with the Taser was shrieking—a soprano now—as I grabbed his neck with both hands, his skin sizzling. Pale goo ate through his collar and muscle in no time, the bastard falling face first to the floor, his limbs jerking and steaming. Caught off guard by my presence (it was clear that nothing here had gone as planned), the other man tightened his grip on Mother, shaking her slender, transfiguring body like a threat.

"Don't come any closer, bug."

Half of Mother's face sloughed away, her round left eye regarding me with the glitter of a million hexagons. The flash of a purple sky.

No, Mother. Don't.

Mother was the imago. I, the worm. Shit, she'd crossed worlds to bring me here, to Cinder, Idaho. Nowhere. Who knows the sacrifices she'd made? She wasn't about to stop now. With a squelch of parting flesh, her maw grew wider, viscera and fluid slopping on the rug. Long and slick, her proboscis whipped out, flailing like licorice lace over her shoulder and shooting up her assailant's nose. Uncoiled, it was down the man's throat in seconds, the meat of him drawn to its glistening length.

And his *essence* too, what humans like to call a 'soul' but we regard as substance. *Strength.* He was still screaming (in my mind, at least) as his chest caved in, his ribs cracking under her immense suction, the otherworldly fury of the Brood. I blinked and his neck was looking like a wrung bath towel. His eyes came popping out of his skull. One of them landed on the couch, wet and bloody. The iris was wide, observing his own undoing. Mother drained him like a pouch of Kool-Aid, his skin wrinkling, dry.

In the madness, I'd forgotten about the woman, the agent. I was powerless when it came to time. Even so I was lurching forward, meaning to grab the gun in her hand. Well, it *looked* like a gun. The muzzle was strange, an opaque bulb that pulsed twice and exploded with light, the walls of the living room shuddering. The shadows cringed and me along with them, shielding my face and hitting the deck, the coffee table legs snapping under me. *Ouch.* My head burned in the radiance. A high-pitched whining skewered my ears. I heard Mother scream, a brief, shattering song. Then bits of her skull were landing on me, her brains decorating the walls, the floor. The lampshade. Whatever heat the Watcher had unleashed, it had proved too much for—

Mother...?

When the shadows pooled back in, the agent was on her knees, cussing and fumbling with the weapon. Mother lay in a heap beside her, her wings dull and unmoving. Her tongue slack, without a head.

Mother!

"Please." This from the remaining Watcher. The Exterminator. An agent of the Cult of Unseen Stars. She couldn't seem to get the weapon to work. She forgot all about it as I rose from the ruins. The blood. "You don't understand," she yelled. Garbled. "The Brood. You're gonna..." The Watcher was gasping, beginning to hyperventilate. "It's *our* world," she sobbed. "You'd do the same."

I took a step toward her. Her jaw hung wide. Purple reflections shone in her eyes.

Before she could scream, I beat her to it.

My first notes. The song of the swarm.

The Watcher was like glass before me. I shattered every window in the house.

THE DREAM WAS OVER. Or rather, the dream had turned into something else. An *expectation.* A ticking clock. For a day I waited, but nobody came. If anyone on Gannett Street had noticed the cars or heard all the ruckus, they'd either run away or they knew better than to interfere. I suspected the latter. Mother had put some kind of trance on the neighbours, I think, spraying spores along with her roses. Or gazing at them over the fence until they found they couldn't look away.

No one dialed 911. No more cars showed up, black or otherwise. I was left with the death in the house.

Damn it, I wanted to go see Tiger so badly. He was my anchor now Mother was gone.

"I love you," I told the darkened house.

To the bodies in the living room, I said, "I wish things could've been different." I said this before I bent to consume them. Mother wouldn't have wanted to go to waste. She was the sweetest of all.

Shit, I wish *I* could've been different, but a glorious purpose was a glorious purpose. It left no room for regret.

And there was… something else going on. Another kind of pull. In my mind, in the whirlwind of screams from the Watchers, shocked, disbelieving and in pain, I kept seeing Craters, up there in the preserve. The volcanic hills and the black plains that for all their bleakness were nothing like the landscape under the skies of home. Not long now. I could feel it in my bones. The throb of my antennae. The stench of every secretion. The flaking of my skin and the slowing of my system. Not long and I'd make my way up there, sing the song that Mother had taught me. Tear at the skin of the world, the membrane between us and triumph.

The fluttering was louder now, a constant, furious gyre scratching at the walls of reality. Praise the Nest. The swarm was ready. The Hour of Emergence was at hand.

"I wish you'd come," I said to the webs that covered everything, the strands that stretched from wall to wall in the hallway, the bedroom, the kitchen. Mother had been busy. Mother had prepared everything.

Know what's sad? Despite my body and my head and my purpose, my heart was beating for Tiger Perez. Tiger in his tight football pants. Tiger with the diamond grin. Tiger under the drowning trees. Was his skin as smooth as the silk between my hands as I wove it back and forth? I thought so. Its stickiness was a reminder that to touch Tiger would be to risk everything. But as I wrapped the stuff around me, again and again and again, I began to look at things in a different way.

I'm not like the other boys. I felt so sleepy as my grey and withered body sank into the warmth of the cocoon, the pupa that Mother had told me about, slipping into incubation and unknown dreams. It was a kind of death, sure, but not forever. At the same time, something bright and sharp was twisting inside. A seed. A worm. A week, a month, no more than that, and the purple would claim me completely. The chrysalis would crack and the new me Emerge. An imago, according to Mother. Emerge and take flight. Go to the plains and herald a new age.

I'm coming out.

Cinder, Idaho, hadn't gone anywhere. Tiger was downtown, I guess. Probably pumping gas. Maybe he'd ask around, find out where I lived. Come to the house looking.

Will he still think I'm special? I wondered.

It was my last waking thought.

Will he find me beautiful?

ECLIPSE, OR THE COURTSHIP OF THE SUN AND MOON

PERRY RUHLAND

The last and final time I attended a performance of the Ballet Fantastique, the title on the bill read *Eclipse, or the Courtship of the Sun and Moon*. The meager troupe, which up until the incident I had considered the finest artistic collective in the city, was based in a shuttered cinematheque on the outskirts of old town, and specialized in the performance of obscure ballets with romantic, often-times fantastical, narratives. While there was an undeniable charm to be had in its maudlin tales of princes and fairies, the main draw of the Ballet Fantastique was the workings of the troupe itself, whose immense talent was matched only by their eccentricity.

From the moment of their conception (the exact date of which none can agree), very little was known about the troupe, and few details offered ever managed to hold up to scrutiny. Eventually, a collective rumor settled, alleging the Ballet Fantastique was somewhat of a fraternal organization —a tight-knit society of highly artistic gentlemen who lived in the shadows, operating in Byzantine codes and rituals. Given their bizarre methods, it made a strange sort of sense. Of the troupe, only three were ever identifiable, albeit to a narrow degree. There were the two anonymous danseurs: a sadistic youth, whom I had previously seen as the lead in some of the troupe's more outre performances, and a massive Russian, whose poise and grace was so great that even his own beauty couldn't outshine his skill. Of the two, I preferred the Russian; tall, limber, lantern-jawed, the perfect form and stature for all of the troupe's many dashing princes, gallant knights, and Grecian heroes. Leading the duo was the illusive composer Herr D., who was only ever glimpsed by way of a pair of shining white gloves jutting out from the darkened orchestra pit. While this elaborate devotion to ritual and performance ensured the Ballet Fantastique was never among the more popular entertainments in the city, it also earned them a slim but devoted following, of which I considered myself a member.

Ever since I had discovered the Ballet Fantastique's existence some years ago, I had made it a point to attend every program the troupe put on, even at times attending multiple performances of the same ballet if the show was particularly strong. Of course, they were all strong, in their own way— for me, to be in the audience of the Ballet Fantastique was to be rocketed from our scum-pond world into one of limitless beauty, where men and music suspend the setting sun just so above the crystal seas, and the heavens above were pure as diamonds.

I fully admit that by the time I witnessed the horrors of that decisive 'Eclipse,' regular attendance of the Ballet Fantastique had become something of a prerequisite for my emotional well-being, and thus when I reached the shuttered cinematheque that dim autumn evening I felt the accumulative pressure of the week's sorrows already growing light. I had arrived early, per usual, and joined a coiling line of fellow devotees beneath the crooked marquee. It was bitter and cold that evening, and the sky was smothered by a sheet of charcoal clouds. I shivered. In a rush to flee my workplace a few hours prior I had neglected to retrieve my overcoat, which now hung in some darkened closet. Still, the chill was preferable to returning off company time, so I sulked in line, content to watch the cherry-red lettering of MOON flicker above me.

~

BY DUSK, the doors opened. The lobby was unchanged from when I had first begun to attend the ballet, and I could only assume that it hadn't been renovated since the cinematheque shuttered early last century. The formerly purple carpet was a blanket of peeling hickory, the lights buzzed at an unbearable frequency, and the rafters served as frames to rich cobweb tapestries. It all felt something akin to home. I made my exchange with the ticket taker (grey, sallow, perpetually mute) and headed into the theater proper.

The theater was spacious, and like the rest of the cinematheque, engaged in a steadily sliding state of disrepair. A majority of the seating was removed, and much of the remaining were obviously broken, sporting splintered backs or seats that jutted up at irregular angles. The entire upper rung of the auditorium was off-limits, and a few of the opera boxes suffered wounds on their undersides, gaping and terminal. Only the curtains that shrouded the mammoth stage appeared to be properly maintained, two billowing sheets of rich twilit blue. Like any self-respecting theatergoer, I had a favorite seat, which I found mercifully, if not expectedly, unattended—five rows from the front, three from the center. I sat, the old fixture groaning beneath me, and waited as the crowd entered.

Per usual, the audience was small enough to only occupy maybe a tenth or less of what the cinematheque could hold in its glory days, and composed largely of misfits—elderly couples in antiquated dress and unaccompanied artistic cynics whose very appearance radiated loneliness. One of them, a woman in her mid-fifties, sat a few seats beside me, brow locked in a permanent furrow. I looked to the blue and let my mind wander to scenes of great beauty, my consciousness buoyed only by the scent of damp wood and the brutal weight of anticipation.

A murmur overtook the theatre, my fantasies fled. Steadily, we were submerged in a pristine dark so thick it rendered even the bitter stranger beside me nothing more than a vague blur. We all sat in shade, I felt my heart beat once, twice. From the shadow, a glow, two iridescent specters breaching the black: the hands of Herr D., bone white gloves wrapped tight around thin, elongated digits with bulbous knuckles. One hand held a gnarled baton, the other was empty. For a moment, they were still. Then, in a single stroke, they sprung to life, and with them the orchestra, invisible in the abyss, their celestial fanfare the roar of a great beast. A silver jolt struck me, a stray breath escaped my lips. Soft lights raised against the curtains, and as the fanfare swelled and my excitement could hardly be contained a moment longer, the pale blue raised on a perfect world.

Behind the curtains was a cosmoscape akin to those found in children's picture books, a black expanse of space painted with purple nebulae and twinkling, many-pointed stars. Conch-shaped galaxies whorled where the high corners met the rafters, and the whole canvas was coated in a kaleidoscopic glitter that stood in for stardust. When the curtains were set, the frenzied intensity of the music ebbed, leaving just the sighs of twin violins, the gentle drone of solar winds. And then, the danseurs.

The first to arrive was the Moon, the lithesome youth, sporting a leotard with a slight grey accent and a bob of silver that nearly covered his eyes. The second, the Sun, was the Russian. His leotard was coated in a dull gold that matched his natural shock of dirty blonde hair, thick black diamonds smudged beneath his eyes. Neither man wore tights, and their rounded calves glistened beneath the stage light. The duo bowed, the dance began.

The ballet consisted of an aggressive pas de deux, the Moon descending upon the Sun in sharp strides and lunges while the besieged star twisted around his blows in a flurry of athletic bounds and shining pirouettes. The strings echoed their movements in the pit below, one violin stabbing while the other wound a retreat. As the dance unfolded in epic, stage-spanning spirals, I found myself stunned. The youth was adept in his role, nimble and with movements that possessed the necessary menace, but the Russian was exemplary, and I began to wonder if I had ever seen him in such a form. As always, he possessed a definite valiance and strength, but tonight it was clear his hero was overrun, a great warrior who, from the moment of his entrance, was doomed to fail. I found myself gripping the seat with brutal claws.

As I watched the show of straining limbs and rippling muscles, my mind twisted down strange new passageways, hurtling through scenes of subjugation, a gallery of mutilated angels. Without thinking, a clenched hand began to drift from the arm of the chair, and when I came to it had worked its way down to the growing excitement in my lap. I surveyed the dark. The audience, elderly couples and artistic cynics alike, were wholly lost in the black. The impression of the woman seated beside me—likely the only one who would notice any improper conduct—stared blankly at the performance, so still she may as well have been inanimate. My hand dipped beneath fabric.

The dance continued. The music had grown more frantic, and the Sun was now the definite loser of the battle, his rasping movements displaying the sort of pathetic weakness only the most accomplished danseur could intentionally conjure. As the violins crescendoed, the youth lunged forth and clasped the Russian's wrists, pulling his muscular arms back while leaning in against his shoulder, and as I attended to myself I saw, or perhaps imagined, canine teeth digging into the taut veins of a supple neck, a crystal tear streaking down a concave cheek. I watched the Russian fail to break the grasp, legs trembling, ankles braced, a shimmer coursing beneath his rear and under his arms. I pictured him bare, tatters of gold stuck to his sweat-matted skin like stardust, and there I would be the Moon, the cruel gem of heaven, descending on him with ropes and whips and knives. Now the hands of Herr D. waved the baton like a mad magician, and the players in the pit swelled with the incantation: low brass rumbling, chimes shrieking, the sound of war. By the time the full orchestra made its return the Sun had well and truly fallen, the Russian splayed out onto his back. The Moon knelt and pulled him close, and I saw in pantomime silver blades on golden skin, and behind my eyes appeared the exquisite suffering of a saint, and the stage swelled with rivulets of red. I strained, gasped, felt myself tighten. I braced for release.

IT NEVER CAME. My eyes flicked back, and in the corner of my vision I glimpsed a pale flicker, a vague shadow trembling. I withered. There, in the upper leftmost corner of the stage where the coral galaxies met the rafters, was a shape veiled beneath a mossy green cloud. At first, I saw it as some abhorrent creature, a mutant animal with a rounded body and a long, protruding appendage, but after a moment I was able to recognize it as the vague silhouette of a human head and an accompanying outstretched arm. Only its hand, wrinkled and white, pierced through the fog. The face was indiscernible.

Only then did I realize that the horrible green had built

steadily in the theater for quite some time now, and when I looked back to the stage I found the fog had grown so thick that it wholly obscured the painted cosmos, giving the odd impression that the stage extended back into an unknown and previously unseen dark. Even the danseurs looked different within the miasma, their skin curdled into some sallow film, their eyes and mouths rendered obscure, sickly pools. Mortified, I looked back to the rafters, where I found the stranger's hand engaged in the same wild, erratic motions of the gloved Herr D. below, claws contracting and pulsing like a swimming jellyfish. Now I saw clearly the silver threads which coiled around the figure's thin fingers, weblike wires that descended from the rafters to the stage, and as I followed the trail down, I felt my stomach sink, for I knew where they would end.

The silver strings were wrapped around the Russian, one pair coiling around his forearms while two more bound his calves, and another still constricted his stomach in peculiar twisting patterns. I watched, dismayed, as he and his partner continued to dance to some new ungodly composition, and as the duo whorled amongst the sickly mist, I understood the horrors of that which I had long adored. Even through the obscuring fog I could recognize that the Russian's act was no act at all, his hollow face twisted into an encapsulation of agony, the abject terror of some small, beaten animal. I knew then too that the 'sadistic' youth was in fact a victim of the same fate, and that the captive duo's dance was nothing but the wild flailing of marionettes carved from flesh and bone. Then it all fell apart, and I understood that the hollow, luminescent gloves of the mysterious Herr D. were all there ever was of the phantom composer, that the orchestra pit was a screaming void in which no musician had ever been present, and even the stage, the sole beacon of beauty in this temple of decay, was a shadow cast from some black sea whose surface bobbed with fetid algae.

All there was, all there ever had been beyond the glamour, was the ghoul—the lurking terror with the human face, the face that was growing ever so clearer and so familiar. And when I glimpsed the first details of the beast's definition emerging from the haze, the awesome spell that had immobilized me was shattered, and I could hardly suppress a scream as I bolted from my seat and fled out from the dreaming crowd, past the long-abandoned ticket booth, through the doors of the shuttered cinematheque and into the arms of the miserable all-freeing night. For that face, that awful face, could only be my own.

STAGE FIVE CLINGER

NIKKI R. LEIGH

I tell the Hand to pull up the voice memo app on Nadine's phone. She's sleeping. The Temple has walloped her internally so that she's out for longer than last time. I've only just begun my story, and there's still at least ten of us to go, all new additions from the past year.

We're careful not to make too much noise—no errant moans or gasps from our many mouths. Our lips are tightly pulled together, as if glued and zipped and sewn just for good measure. We know that our stories must be heard clearly. Spoken with no interruption.

We don't want to be stuck to her much longer.

The Hand and Arm work together to bring the phone closer to where I am: the Hip. The Hand pushes record, and I open my mouth, stretch my lips and wet my tongue. I speak.

I'm going to start this story at the end of the first night. The beginning of the end, really. The first time I felt simultaneously in control and out of it. Bear with me, it's a windy road, but love—and obsession—usually is. I can admit that now. Can still see it, that first night, circular, replaying. Live it. Try to sleep and can't, so I live it again. Welcome to my thoughts, it's all I have left anyway. Let's go.

~

THREE WEEKS AGO

I'm paralyzed by her.

My face was stuffed somewhere in the crevice of Nadine's shoulder blades. I'm careful not to pull away, for fear of waking her with that unflattering sound and feeling of naked flesh unsticking itself from other naked flesh.

Since I couldn't move and my mind was far from sleep, I let it wander and take adventures, hoping to burn off the excess energy. The buzz of the night. The vibration still humming through my veins. I needed to let it fizz out so I could get some semblance of sleep before work tomorrow.

I yawned, smelling her again as I do. I couldn't help but feel a rumble of excitement, accomplishment, and a bit of anxiety swirl together when I caught that hint of her sex on my face.

It was my first time—with another woman at least—and I never thought that I'd feel so much like a toddler again, my legs wobbly beneath me as I try to navigate new terrain.

I thought about that gaze she sent my way, across tables at the bar, the local lesbian watering hole, from what I had gathered in my Yelp research. Apparently *the* spot for new and old queers. A drink or ten to build up the courage, a feast —of both women and really good sliders if you could stomach the grease.

I'd stared, mouth open, beef spilling out of my mouth when I made eye contact with her. Felt heat flush to my cheeks and my groin and a guttural, audible groan escaped my lips.

"No, no, that one's trouble," Addie said. "I've heard that half the San Francisco girls have been her prey. Do you know how many queer people San Francisco has?"

"Shut up, Addie," I said.

"Why not that one, over there? She's cute and looks safe.

You can probably figure this shit out with her and she wouldn't eat your head off in the process."

I looked over to where Addie was not so inconspicuously pointing. A sweet looking girl in a button up shirt and a cute nose-piercing waved in my direction. I waved back, letting my fingers dance like blades of grass in the wind.

She was pretty, and like Addie had said, probably safe. Not that I knew the first thing about dating girls. And that was my problem, because my ignorant ass seemed to be drawn to the most dangerous girl in the room.

"No, stop it, Suzie. I'm telling you, don't even bother. You know how many hearts she's broken? It'll be whatever that astronomically high number is plus one once she's done with you," Addie said.

I watched the girl lick the excess alcohol from her lips, the honey-colored drink on the rocks making her look goddamn untouchable.

"The heart wants what the heart wants, Addie."

"The heart doesn't want that. Trust me. The loins might, but the heart doesn't."

"Please stop telling me how to gay. It's my gay or the highgay."

"How are we friends?" Addie sighed dramatically.

"I'm going to the bathroom. Want me to bring back a drink?"

She smiled. "Ah yes, that's why we're friends. Margarita please. A double, if I'm going to have to watch you make ogley-eyes at her all night."

I smacked Addie's shoulder and headed to the bathroom, which had a line of dancing queers that nearly reached the bar. Yet another unforeseen drawback of dating at the local lezzie bar: ridiculously long waits for the restroom.

I really did have so much to learn.

I tapped my foot impatiently on the sticky ground of the bar floor. My eyes darted around the room, falling on the array of missing posters behind the bar. At least a dozen faces, all young women, were tacked up on the wall along with the number for the local LGBTQ+ Community Center. I remember thinking that was odd—you'd think I'd have heard of a group of young women who'd recently disappeared before that moment.

I tried to note their faces, but they were blurring together from the alcohol buzzing through my veins. I turned my attention to the rest of the room. All around me, women were coupling up, eyes glazed over from alcohol, discarded plates forgotten beside them. There were new dishes each night, served hot, after all. The soft glow of string lights hanging from the wooden rafters made it all seem so idyllic. So normal. Maybe one day I'd find my peace here, but for now, I was overstimulated and stressed from its newness.

The line shuffled forward. With too much time spent waiting to release my bladder, I found my mind drifting to how I got to this spot. This oversexed bar with these over-horny people, in over my horny head. I didn't even know I *was* horny for other women a week ago.

Hardy-har, right? The thirty-year-old who finally figured things out after forced and failed relationships and a near giving up on love. How could I not have realized? Not have known?

I could probably overanalyze my sexual orientation-based misgivings until the cows came home, but I'll just settle on this: I didn't know, until I did. Just kind of struck my mind like a flick to the forehead one night, lying in bed with too much anxiety swirling in my brain. It struck me, it settled, and since then, the rest of me just fell into place.

And then I was there. In the bar. Apparently with a taste for the most off-limits girl in this humid, loud place.

The line shifted again.

A voice in my ear caused me to almost piss my pants.

"Hive mind urination, am I right?" I jumped a bit more

than I would have liked in front of the girl I'd been making lovestruck eyes at not five minutes earlier. Addie's warning echoed in my mind. I ignored it.

"You've surely got a better pick-up line than that?" I fired back, hoping to sound as cool as I wished I was.

She laughed, the sound like a rainbow arcing over the loud music in the bar. Ugh, even my intrusive thoughts are gay.

"Who says I was trying to pick you up?"

"Everyone does, you just can't hear it over this abysmally loud bass drop."

"You're right, my mistake. In that case, do you have plans later?"

And that was all she wrote. My naïve, fresh-lesbian soul felt like it had mated. Within the hour, I had left the bar with Nadine and was making my way up the steps of her apartment complex and into her bedroom and clothes were off and we were having sex and I was becoming whole. My whole world was vibrating and sending out ripples of color. I tried to let my instincts take over, remembered what felt good for me, see if it felt good for her.

I didn't tell her it was my first time. I didn't want to scare her off. But somehow, she knew, I learned, panting naked and slippery with sweat later that night.

"Pretty good for the first go at it," Nadine had said. "You going to stay the night? I've been told I snore."

I was still feeling whammed by the realization that I was exposed and revealed to be the complete newbie I was.

"I...I can stay," I stuttered out.

"Just don't get too attached or anything. We can spoon, but I'm not really looking for anything serious."

I couldn't think of a response that wouldn't make me sound any less like the loser that I was, so I settled on latching onto her back, draping an arm over her midsection, and trying to sleep.

She didn't say another word, and my mind was racing. I don't think I slept a wink that night, nor any of the nights since. I sighed. *See? We've been here before.*

I started the night over in my mind again.

$\approx$

THAT'S HOW WE MET, so I'll tell you how we ended. I'm not sure I can continue tonight though. The sun is starting to come up and wheezing out these words has taken more out of me than I thought it would.

We're all in agreement, the Hand and Arm, and I, the Hip. We shut the phone off, place it back where it was as Nadine begins to stir.

Crisis averted. I know our mouths will seal when she awakens. Disappear when she regains control, and we'll revert to our place in the trunk, forgotten as she goes about her day. As I let myself fall back into her, I almost shout with what little energy I have left. I can feel her hunger, her need to consume. Maybe she'll go out again and gather another one of us. Her knee is looking rather bare these days.

$\approx$

IT'S a few nights later now. She's asleep again, and her bed is finally empty. She had a girl over the last two evenings, and I can only hope she's strong enough to fight the lure Nadine exudes. We couldn't, and we're paying that price.

The Temple, Arm, Hand and I work at it again, setting up the phone so I can tell the rest of my story. It'll be their turn soon, if this works out, and I know they're excited to use a voice they'd lost months ago.

Alright, the rest of my story. I started with the beginning of my end, so allow me a bit of meandering now so I can explain how I turned into nothing but a puckered mouth that only breathes when she's asleep.

~

ONE WEEK AGO

I found her at that bar again. A solid seven days had passed since we had sex for the first time, and my *first* kind of first, and I hadn't stopped thinking about her since. The morning after my inaugural trip down under, I made her coffee, eggs, awkwardly fixed my hair and pressed my clothes under my palms as she sauntered to the table. She had this look of pain in her eyes, like she could see what was happening and wanted nothing to do with it.

"Thanks...what's your name again?" At least she was honest.

"Suzie." My cheeks flushed.

"Suzie, right. Look, don't take this personally, but this isn't going to be a thing. Unless, you know, you're okay with just the sex."

I looked at her longingly.

"I'm not opposed to the sex, you know. You were pretty good. I'm just not looking for commitment. You've got that look like you're ready to lay down roots here in my apartment. Like you skipped stages one and two and hopped right into stage three. Don't. You wanted a good, easy first time, right?"

I think this is the most I've heard her speak since we've met. I stayed silent.

"So, you got it. Easy, no strings attached."

"Okay," I finally said. "Okay."

"Alright, glad that's sorted," Nadine said through a smile.

I excused myself, went straight to work in last night's clothes, reeking of alcohol.

"Sorted" she had said. I couldn't help but feel used. I spent the next few days thinking about just how used I had felt until all of a sudden that feeling of being yesterday's garbage finally got taken out to the dumpster and I seemed to forget my torment.

I found her at that bar. We went back to her apartment. We had sex.

We did it again the next night, too. I craved the way my hands seemed to find holds everywhere in her body, like I was climbing a rock wall and she was the path. It felt like I was slipping into her, becoming her when she reached her peak; we'd climb Everest together, flesh and flesh.

Each time she finished it was an orchestra of moans and screams. It sounded like she was everywhere at once, and for a second, I wondered if she had an extra mouth hidden somewhere.

I lay nestled into her back again, thinking about her dimples, her laugh, and how much of a woman she was. And that was really something to me. She was a *woman* and I was a *woman* and I couldn't get over the fact that we had been together in that way, after spending a whole life not realizing just how amazing it could be.

The next day at work, Addie pressed for information, teased me for falling in deep. Said she could see it written all over my face like I'd fallen asleep first at a party and someone had scribbled "this bitch is in love" in Sharpie across my forehead.

But she was right. I couldn't believe it. A week and a half, and my heart was hammered, drunk with Nadine.

I texted her that night. "Can I take you out?"

"Drinks?"

I tried to be bold, texted: "Dinner???"

There was a long pause of blinking ellipses on the screen as she typed. "No strings remember?"

I breathed, chose my words carefully so I could get what I wanted: "No strings, just burgers."

Another long pause, but she agreed to meet me at the restaurant next to my favorite park where I planned to win her over under the stars.

We met, we ate, I paid, and made some excuse about walking the food off. She didn't protest, claiming to need the fresh air herself.

We walked, moonlight illuminating the way. I tried to grab her hand, but she shoved it in her pocket. I tried to kiss her, but she turned her cheek.

I longed for her touch, and she seemed to want to be anywhere but with me, her phone buzzing occasionally in her pocket. She stopped walking, turned to face me.

"Please don't ask me to be your girlfriend."

I sputtered, feeling called out and ashamed. She turned down the thing I wanted and I hadn't even asked her.

"Look, Suzie, you seem real nice and all. You're going to make some girl really happy. But that girl isn't me. I promise you that."

"But how do you know?"

She sighed. "I see this all the time. The first girl you sleep with, that one that basically reorients the rest of your life, it makes you fall in deep. You can't help it. I try not to make a habit of sleeping with the newly gay, but you were so forward in that line to the bathroom I didn't think you were."

"Can't you just pretend I'm not?"

"That's beside the point. It doesn't matter what I want, it's what you *think* you want."

I was trying not to cry.

"I'm not worth it," Nadine continued. "Do you know why my phone keeps ringing? It's my on-again, off-again girlfriend asking if I got my free dinner from the Stage Five Clinger."

"Ouch," I said, wincing internally more than I let on, trying to mask the utter raw pain.

"This girl, she's my puppeteer. When you and I sleep

together, she's the one I wish it was. You fall, and no matter what, I can't stop you. I'll eat you alive. And I'll smile the whole time."

I could see what she was doing, being needlessly cruel. It was working.

"I get it," I said. "You can stop."

"I'm sorry."

"Can we still...you know?"

She laughed. "You do have those talented fingers. Just a fuck?"

I nodded my head, weighed down by the lump in my throat. "Just a fuck."

And we did.

I lied to myself as much as I lied to her. For another week I tried. Just the physical. Grunts late into the night. I wouldn't stay over, but rather gather my clothes and shuffle off for long night drives wishing I wasn't doing exactly what I was doing.

I kept having sex, because it was the only way I could be with her. It was humiliating, but exhilarating.

I'd stare into her eyes and imagine a lifetime of doing so, and she'd stare back, challenging me. She had all the power, and she knew it. From her coy smiles, I could tell that she liked it. Thrived off it, even as she protested against it. It was a dance she danced often, and she had mastered every step. Every house I imagined us owning together, every kid I imagined cradled in our arms was another card in her voraciously selfish deck.

She was winning every night, but at least they were nights with her.

I was falling in deep. Trying not to let her know. But somewhere within the confines of her hardened shell, her body knew. And it was absorbing me.

Talented fingers and all.

NADINE ROLLS OVER, and I shout at the Temple. Scream at it with my mouth and tongue flapping at her hip to slam a concussive force into her skull and stop her. I'm almost done with this story.

If Nadine learns that we've grown, this whole thing is over and we're back to being trapped.

If she figures out that we've opened like slits across her body at night, that as we remember more about who we are, that we become mouths and speak, we're done. We've learnt about each other each night and want to tell the world about Nadine, the many-mouthed beast.

We can't lose. We have nothing left of ourselves.

The Temple does her job. Nadine is out again. The Hand and Arm reposition the phone by me at her Hip.

My story. The rest of my story.

LAST WEEK

Deeper, harder, faster; I fell. And the night that it happened, that I lost nearly all of myself, I was full of regret.

I remember that first time I saw Nadine, at the bar when Addie told me to choose a different girl, that nice-looking girl. Someone easy and kind and who wouldn't eat me for breakfast. I chose to be a meal, though, I just didn't realize how literal it would be.

I was in her bed when every colossal shit from the past month hit the fan at warp speed. I found myself doing something I had promised myself I wouldn't do.

I was crying into Nadine's back, clinging to her tight.

"I'm sorry," I sobbed, ashamed that I couldn't help the attachment I felt.

"Oh, Suzie. I didn't want this for you."

"It's not like you didn't warn me."

"Yeah, about that—"

"I just can't help it. You're so great and everything."

"I'm really not."

"You are, and I don't think I'll ever find anyone like you."

"Please don't say that," she said, and for the first time I heard fear in her voice.

"What's wrong? Why are you so resistant to this?"

Nadine's body tensed, and in that moment, I felt a shift within her. She started to sweat, and my arms wrapped around her body had become soaked with her. I knew that if I didn't act fast, this might be the last time I saw Nadine, and I didn't want to lose her. I started to rub her skin with my clammy hands. She told me not to stop. From my position, behind her goosebump-covered frame, I tried to work my way into her, ready to pull her apart with my teeth and lick her wounds with my salted tongue.

She climaxes, fast, and when she does, all of her mouths open.

I stare at the gaping slits. They're close to everywhere: a pair of full-bodied lips on her shoulder, a cleft-lip at her temple, a pinched mouth on her forearm and a toothy mouth on her hand. Mouths, teeth, tongues, everywhere on her exposed skin.

I don't even have time to think about how I never noticed them. Later, once I was assimilated and started seeing it happen to someone else, I realized it's because when you're face-deep in someone, you're not really paying attention to much else. Especially not in *that* moment, when the stars align and the climax triggers.

But here I am, fully aware in her moment of glory and I can see them all, the dozen mouths, all groaning at once, making up a monstrous scream of ecstasy that tumbles from every pair of lips Nadine has.

Then, for the first time in our short-lived relationship or

whatever this was, she turned to me, her voice—*voices?* —hoarse and offered the magical words of reciprocation.

"Your turn," she husked.

I scrambled away from her naked body, her mouths gasping at air, moaning in an off-tempo and out-of-key way that sounded like a whole graveyard of encroaching ghouls.

She grabbed my hand.

"Let me teach you. You just place your hand here, and I'll do the rest."

I hated that I was so turned on by her still, with the mouths on her body aching for air, aching to scream again. She was finally giving back, and I just wanted it so badly that I didn't even notice when my fingertips started sinking into her skin, through it, as if her very pores were inviting me in.

"Stage Five," she said, when I finally realized I was wrist deep in her hip, my flesh fused to hers.

She reared her head back, and all her mouths smiled.

"Now *cling.*"

And with that, I was lost. I could do nothing to pull away, my body sinking inch by inch, folding and melting into her own. I funneled into her bones, her flesh, her blood, and became as much her as anything else.

I felt myself disperse into her, stuck on everything inside, my entire existence squashed into hers. Sucking and squeezing and breaking and realigning filling every gap in her already crowded body.

I finally had what I wanted, attached at the hip. I wondered if Addie would miss me. I'd been kind of a shitty friend for the last few weeks.

I hoped she'd feed my cat.

∿

So THAT'S how I became the Hip. Not all that different than the Arm and the Hand, though the Temple's story is a bit more treacherous, I'm told.

Fell too deep, and now we're stuck. Forever falling, nothing but flesh around us to cushion the blow.

The Hand taps the phone to end the recording. My story is over. It took us a while to figure out how to navigate Nadine's body while she was sleeping. But when we did, we reached for the phone. We hit record. We spoke.

Tomorrow, a new story. Until then, our lips seal together, we recede, and we wait.

THE LOVE THAT WHIRLS

JOE KOCH

*J*ohn dances, graceful as a rhinoceros. Boys circle him like flames. Illuminated by the candles in their hands, writhing to the repeated track, their flickering faces wear every expression from certified indifference to the green hustler's triumphant smirk.

Jaded or gleeful, it all depends on where they fall in their journey as prostitutes. Falling is the mutual journey ending in our semi-sacred circle tonight, though I don't know this until after the tragic end. John has the stupidest accident of his stupid wasted life that night. Stupid John, with his fear of freedom, fear of heights. Falling and fawning, all of us prostitute imposters, mimicking the enslavement we crave to spin us senselessly around the one elusive thing we want.

No one warns you there's nothing in the center of the storm except vacant, still air. This is the work of death: love under will, burying what you've unmade. Here: take my hand and I'll show you the full process when we get to the part with the lost footage.

That's what you came here to see, isn't it?

Meanwhile, enjoy the dancing boys, topless, of course. The tallest and oldest of them, the one I'll be spending all my money on at the bar later tonight, can barely be bothered to make eye contact with the camera. He's aging out of his profession and later tonight I will use him in a way that will cut his career short. I like pushing boys who've seen too much to open up a little bit wider. That's the reason they go looking in the first place. I respond to what people want. I care about the boys I fuck. The oldest and tallest one's instinctive aversion to my penetrating lens is the opposite of John, who I have protected from the things he fears.

John can't peel his obsequious eyes away from the camera long enough to enact a seductive tease. He's not my ideal body type, overweight and overdressed in the middle of the sacrificial circle, surrounded by beautiful dancing boys bearing candlelight. John gapes like an amazed infant. If eyes could drool, his would.

"Canter about and do a little spin for me, love. There you go." I demonstrate the desired motion with my wrist. John puzzles out the idea after a lingering gawk of incomprehension. His ignorance is my fault. I've been free-handing out hallucinogenic treats.

His awkwardness, too. John's clumsy twirl endangers the hired help. Shirtless boys back off to accommodate his width and then pulse inward to buoy him aloft, flames a safe distance away. Consummate professionals, they keep John on his mark despite the wavering ineptitude of his turn. Ever an intrusion, I embrace and I smile. John's so pleased with himself it's contagious.

Candlelight illuminates the cave, or so it appears on film. The contrast is dramatic. Edits after the fact will erase what isn't ethereal and sinister in John's fumbling dance. Slender torsos flicker in and out of the liquid darkness around him. Mingling elements of water and fire, wax drips on a flat abdomen. The slathered boy telegraphs his pain tolerance as an aperitif to sex. Raising his flame with calm, he reveals ancient handprints and primeval renditions of horn-headed god-things gathered on the cave walls. Filming here is utterly illegal, of course.

John's face bloats forward, bleached by the beam of the spotlight trained to his head. Framed by a halo he can't shake off. His generous-sized top catches duplicate glimmers on the sequins. The unfortunate effect highlights the pasty insecurity of his looming middle age, the shifting undertones of worry in his dilated green eyes, and the fearful padding of luxury's waste like innocence advertising the wrong kind of childishness to claim good taste.

"No, no," I correct the boys closest to John. Two of the youngest—the cagey ones who agreed to be our guides in finding the caves—reach, grinning, for John's privates and pop open his top buttons.

"That's enough, loves," I repeat with more force.

The boys laugh. John joins in the mirth. A vague understanding they want to pleasure him and an impulsive desire to indulge the professionals in exercising their skill sends his eyes to his crotch as if he's found a new toy to share. Their fondling awakes something playful and missing in John.

Until he remembers me.

His gaze shoots up into my spotlight. He stares, blinded by my approach.

I hate to say he's a deer in the headlights. I like to think I'm more creative and it's such a tired old cliché, but honestly darling. Look at him. *Look.*

John knows what happens when boys misbehave.

When I'm finished with the two cagey twinks and seek to appease John's panic, I'm revolted to realize I've left the camera running. The spotlight rests on the rocky sediment veneer clearly aimed at the surreal carnage. John glares, shaking from an anguished protest launched moments ago, lips still quivering with the sweet spittle that showered me when he screamed to *fucking stop it.* I didn't.

Here's where you can make a clever joke about things on the cutting room floor.

In the face of death and its unreliable permutations, as in the face of rampant desire, one must try to preserve a semblance of humor. To be blunt, and I am nothing if not honest, recording the emotional evisceration appalls me more than capturing the images of physical disruption. You'll understand my position better once you remember where you've seen John before. Yes, he's no stranger, I assure you. What a wonderful surprise you're in for, my darling boy.

Cutting this beast into a coherent narrative was already going to prove a monumental chore given John's lackadaisical performance and poor coordination, and now the film's challenges are further compounded by the need to delete evidence. What a terrible waste of perfectly good body parts.

Add in film stock and all too precious time, and it occurs to me no one in the audience will believe it's real. The most efficient solution is to use the scene as so-called special effects. Thus the footage survived until it was seized by customs. You're the first to view it other than me, the border patrol, and whoever they sell to on the black market when they happen upon a choice piece of violent pornography.

"My god," John says. "What even are you anymore?"

Disgust ruins his good looks. I lecture; a terrible choice. A compulsion I can't quit.

"Cryptids and monsters in film have been queer-coded for decades. Certainly we queers can claim the rights to our own fantastic version of were-coding, by myth or magic or any means necessary. We deserve our own branch of occult evolution. God knows we've taken enough shit from society to earn it."

Surrounded by bare feet except for John's atrocious snakeskin cowboy boots—yes, of course, he just had to have them when we drove through Texas, didn't he?—I rise from the cave floor to reconfigure in an acceptable form without incurring any chemical errors. Cave geology is not my field of study. I've no idea what kind of endemic viruses or fecal deposits might nest invisibly on the ancient sediment. The very thought of fundamentally altering my biology along accidental parameters makes me cringe with dysphoria.

John's guiding enzymes from his outburst help reorganize my shape in a way he tolerates, prefers, and determines, although sweet boy that he is, John's never understood the power he has over me.

I know, I know; too many conundrums. All shall be clear soon enough. Indulge me a little longer, as an elder.

You see, for every transformation, there's a price. I watch the cost deducted from John's eyes this very minute. Dread closes the doors to his soul, locking the child inside.

I learn in retrospect that our reenacted ritual disaster is my fault, every bit of it an intentional mistake based on the false eye in the center of the swirling storm. Everything from feeding John's paunch to inelucticating the damaged boys has sped our leap towards a future that is ending too soon for both of us to reconcile.

A boy like you might call me foolish for finishing a lost film at the end of my life that no one else will ever watch, but what else do you do when you're being swallowed by the clock? What does one do when you're a slimy white swimmer sliding down the throat of time?

Right or wrong, you do what you've always done.

You grab history by the cock and pump every drop of life out of it.

And you do it with vengeance. You do it with love.

～

THE NIGHTMARES START AGAIN after I lose John. Not when I lose him on the way back from the caves due to the unfortunate state of the two boys, and not later at the club where he drinks to excess despite the plentiful drugs I most graciously supply. Not even later that night or the next morning when the world as I know it ends, for there is no world for me without John, none at all. I lose him long before then, when he's right in front of me and smiling.

What's that they say? One may smile and smile and be a villain. But that's not fair to my darling John, is it? I'm the villain, obviously. The monster in the bathroom conservatives keep warning you about. I'm the one who corrupts him as a young lad.

"You're of no use to me sober," I'll say, feeding him some new concoction, much to his hedonistic adolescent delight. His Pentecostal father binges and recovers on a regular basis. Always remorseful, he vows to protect John from the demon rum. A beginner's move against a beginner demon.

Under the shadow of the bullying patriarch, John runs wild. How thrilling to see him then, all blondish tangles and uncontrolled urges. Bartering a fistful of mundane tablets in exchange for a bottle, he stalks strangers outside the corner store. He swerves out of the alley, almost crashing into me. The gentle voice accosts with more power than his crass physicality. My scalp tingles.

"Hey, mister, do you need something?"

His eyes hit me at close range. "Oh, I'm sorry, ma—"

"No, no," I rush to interrupt. "Don't apologize. You were right the first time."

John wipes his nose with the back of his free hand. He uses the same hand to push the hair out of his eyes before wiping it off on his jeans. He proffers his questionable wares. "Do you, um?"

I wave off his palm. "Put that silly trash away. Not that I'm opposed to decongestants and baby aspirin. What have you got there, expired Percocet? No thank you, love. Now look, what can I get for you? My treat."

"I'm, uh, not into, you know."

He nods at my abdominal area. My chest. Shrugs and looks hopeful. "Okay?"

I stretch my arms wide. The tails of my embroidered frock coat spread wide and flap in the steely wind, making a pleasant, watery sound. Winter nears, when the veils fall away and the snow blindness of mental cessation lulls our most secret longings out into the open to wander.

In the dead of winter, how we wander and pine. I say, "Behold a great mystery. Herein lie bones made of impermanent stuff, matter most fluid, a formless form capable of intertwining the many scattered puzzle pieces which compose the formulas of your desire. Does the sand rattle in the hourglass, or is the hourglass made of boiled and blown sand? We too are boiled and blown, and our hidden bones rattle corporeal in this dark alley on this dark night. What if the answer is not one or the other, but both, depending upon factors of heat, pressure, and resistance? Tell me, what do you desire?"

His eyes dart as if he seeks a spy. As if he's meant for me. "Hey, look. I'm cool. I'll just—"

"There's no need for resistance. You can have anything you want. Where's the harm? My answer is yes."

He scoffs. Then he speaks a wish and I grant it.

Swigging from the overpriced bottle, John fails to suppress a crafty and satisfied smile. "Thanks, fairy godmother."

"Call me *Daddy*. Would you like to come home with me?"

John coughs. "Whoa, hold on."

"I apologize." I hold up both hands and back up.

His arm stretches toward me with the bottle in his grip. "You said it wasn't like that. Here."

I don't take it. Poor dear, I've spooked him. I say, "Where are my manners? Keep what's yours, please. As you see, I've been inhabiting an all too private niche for an excessive length of time."

"You're a what?"

"Let's just say my last relationship ended badly."

John looks down the empty street as he tips back the bottle. His hair blows in the opposite direction of his gaze. Scars circle the edge of his left brow. The green tint of healing bruises blooms on his cheek. Sour apples have always been my favorite.

"Is it nice, or some sort of dungeon?" John says, still looking away.

The cool wind encircles us, mingling our animal odors and mystical fates. The rest of the city aches with jealousy and emptiness.

I nudge the dull cardboard layered beneath the open lid of the liquor store dumpster with the shiny tip of my boot. "Well, what do you call this?"

When I rise later to leave him where we've sat on the curb adjacent to the alley, John also rises, emptying the bottle. Golden hair like the sun transgressing into forbidden night. Territory of the moon inverted, I lead him with gifts, but it is John's will we follow from that moment and ever after to the end. John's will is an autonomous angel, a living relic he forgets.

I want you to understand something. It's important. I never had anything but his best interests at heart.

Because what if your body was a lie you believed for more than half a century? When you started taking it apart, you'd undo the structures of every part of the world that was once familiar and reliable. You'd unravel the strings cementing reality and expose the very cement as strings; the strings as phantoms; the phantoms as the blank stillness of dead air inside a whirlwind of external deceptions. You'd know nothing.

Making love to John is less about pleasure than about learning to exit margins.

In time, despite his petty thefts and moody defections from my care, my chemical synthesis erodes the previous form and realigns. John begins to trust me when the tips of encrusted wings sprout from my shoulder blades, when my skin tone deepens to match the pigments of stone he admires in the museum. Never certain how a lover's expectations will morph me, intimate seclusion with John induces tourmaline seizures and the surprise retention of breasts.

I'm careful not to complain about the excruciating pain. I endure ongoing and contradictory physiological transformations. After all, I don't want to scare him off. I'm not sure John knows what he wants or how his mercurial desires fluctuate dangerously. Again and again he flees from me and returns. I wait in patient self-isolation, a monk mutating to fit his inmost desires.

Crashing into the bedroom drunk and angry, John leaps on my back as I sleep. He smells like his father. I know because by now I interweave with his memory. Fearful self-loathing shakes his long-fingered hands. One claims a grip around my throat and the other tears at my lavishly spiked wings. He ravages the slick feathers and pumps my windpipe with a grossly masturbatory thumb.

His hand crawls to my mouth. Five fingers pass through the hole between my lips and fist my palate, testing my gag reflex. John pants as if he's finishing a sprint. He hardens against my back.

Abruptly, his fist pulls out. He cups his palm under my mouth. "Spit."

For the first time between us, John takes control.

In the midst of an ecstasy of fullness, I'm bereft. John is gone. Absolution is lost to me. I'm alone even while gripping him and bleeding for him, even as these violent transformations respond and recalibrate my structure to meet his uncertain needs. I grow a beak: long, sharp, curved, and metallic. It falls off. My feathers turn to tongues. He bites them, and they blink into ash. John sets fire to the many-headed corkscrew of skeletal genitalia I've grown for him. He screams as the milky flames lick his eyes like acid. The ceiling drips. I dissolve into a worm of muscle made only to suck.

I'll survive. I'll grow back. I'll take him when it's my turn and spin John-the-very-bad-dancer around and around, whirling like the cosmological pattern of a nearby galaxy or the spiraled layers of muscle constructing the Mobius strip of the human heart. This is our mutual dance, even though I know I've lost him in that moment. I won't let go.

Take my hand again and I'll show you what it feels like.

Is it worth it? All that effort for one brief spin?

Once John's had his way, I cradle him in the shreds of my mangled wings. Armless, I enfold his sweat and tear-stained face to suckle at my stone-carved breast. There's nothing there for him. I'm a statue, after all. John's warm quivering cheek cools against my polished surface. Smooth rock resists intimacy.

The nightmares start again that night, drifting as we embrace into dawn. Dreams hold me immobile in a dress made of concrete poured by my father. I don't remember the man. John sleeps in peace now that he's channeled his inner patriarch through my core and out the other side like liquid coal. I dream for both of us, jealous of John's erotic monster.

Kill all kings, kiss all kings. We won't evade sacrifice once we claim sovereignty over the deadly spiral of biological time.

~

It's nothing but an accident. That's the ruling, though it's hard for me to accept. I revisit the night it happens every time I watch this footage. Notice how he's crippled me slowly in anticipation, plucked my feathers down to corroded nubs. After all these years with John, a tail hangs thick between my legs, anchoring me to the immobile club floor. Thwarting a crowd of boys in the post-cave party, a sparkling demiurge in the disco, John dives over a ledge, usurper of true kings.

We all wish to be thus canonized in our pristine moment of truth. What the mind reveals as one careens downward to the end must be like a wild trick of the light. Get close enough to death and the lies should be blown away in a flash, don't you think?

Don't you think it must be like that?

John knew what he wanted for once. He lived in that flame.

Who am I to change his course? Nothing but the old creep who keeps him in his cups, distracted in the moment of crisis by the tall jaded dancer from the caves going down on me in a crowded stall. The walls shake. John's desire is like blood. It burns as it flows in an imitation of a disease through my system, a consequence of our long union, a hot curse bursting from every sore in my augmented organ.

The boy spits me out in disgust. Thick crimson smears his face. It's too much for him. The taste of true love dying in his mouth.

The crash, the shrieks from the dance floor, the boys above, gawking at the failed railing and darting away from the scene of the crime with the feral instinct of a dog pack. I see it from every angle as I come in the jaded boy's gagging mouth. The pain of each physical thrust that roots me deeper in a stranger's affronted trench matches the flashing pictures of John's clumsy plunge.

A medical anomaly, they say later. He didn't fall very far. Quite an unusual way to die, the medical examiner tells me with an admiring sort of pride in his tone.

I stare at him, struggling to connect this assessment to any reality in which I can willingly participate. "Yes," I say with a stammer. "He's a most unusual boy."

In the examiner's surprise and disdain I read his unspoken corrections: *was*, and *hardly a boy*.

His attentive hesitation unnerves me. "I'm sorry," I say. "I've never..." He turns, and I wonder later if I was supposed to give him a tip.

I awake in a bed that smells of John's living body. When they asked if I wanted more time alone with the corpse I said no. That limp carcass laid out on the table wasn't John. Its uncanny similarity made John's absence too palpable. I felt rage. I wanted to kick the giant puppet and beat its lies back into the nonexistence it represented. I wanted to scream at John to come back and stop his fucking childish games. I couldn't touch the awful thing, couldn't look at it.

Turning away in an empty bed, wrongness in the faint light of dawn darkens, drawing down the veil of the unreal. My racing heart surges into my throat where it stops beating. I'm glad of it, glad to be dead. Or perhaps it beats so hard it's exploding: pounding, fluttering with torn wings like a moth turning into powder mid-flight. I choke on the dust.

I'm falling. I can't see.

My body plummets as my heart skips and stops like excitement, like death. I'm tied down by silky wet tendrils strapping me to the bed erotically, and yet somehow I'm also plunging down an endless gulch. I'm pleading with John from a dark compass point inside my blacked-out unspun head.

I didn't mean those things.

What more can I do to please you? Haven't I given you everything?

Oh, the boys. You know they don't matter to me.

If death is all there is, take me with you.

Take me down with you. Make it hurt.

I can't cry. Grief is a black hood cinched over my head. I lift the clay weight of my limbs like a kidnap victim immobilized for days.

This isn't what we planned. This isn't the magic we worked toward. This body is a failed organism.

This film is a question that cuts my throat.

Cloven through the paper trachea, a spot most vulnerable, artifact of my love made incontinent. Opened arteries soak the thin tissue lining of my layered and aging skin, stains splitting into halves, tearing a blood infused seam in the shape of a child's Valentine's card heart.

Paper is all I'm made of. See how easily I fold into an origami simulation of a mythical winged beast? See how I spin on a transparent thread and flutter helpless upon invisible currents when it is cut?

See me now for what I am, John: folded together, a dance of intersecting paper angles and duplicating planes. Tuck me into your center. Cross your heart with false hope. Press my sections in place with bone and tweezers. Flex flat the seams of both mountain and valley tessellations, for I agree to fall with you. The reverse and inverse exacting a pattern; perplexing until we unfold like blooming crystals, like the thick substance of the beloved, like the antithesis of all that is lost.

Here is my hand, John. Reach out, grab hold, and come back to me.

ANYWAY.

The lost footage. That's what you really want to see, isn't it? It's your only possible motive for letting me carry on so.

You're too sweet. More than sweet, in fact. Past the point of ripe to rottenness.

No, don't let go. Hold my hand firm, darling. Feel the

pressure of my flesh against what's left of yours while we finish our screening. Let me fondle your exposed glove of bone. If I hold you long enough the film won't be a story anymore. It will become part of you. Flesh and blood.

The thing you can't foresee about shape-shifting and taking apart other people's bodies is the absolute compliance of temporal flesh. The way it bends to strong intention. Killing isn't an act of violence. No more than being born. You'll forgive me for being a novice at both.

When I was born, I had to chew my way out into this world or die suffocated by a prolapsing uterus and its strangling tentacle cord of umbilicus. No one helped me. I survived by devouring my own death. Do you believe I can resurrect you by devouring yours? Do you feel new movement yet in your desiccated flesh?

Your hard on says yes. Though your bulge may be a bloated sac of corpse flies ready to hatch, I'm going to give you the benefit of the doubt as long as I can stomach your rank odor. Does some glimmer of recognition infuse beneath the shredded fabric of your burial suit? Do your blonde wisps curl with invigorated growth? Do you remember me yet? Do you remember yourself?

Yes is always the right answer. I understand, though, if you're not quite ready to speak, darling John. I do hope you appreciate the expense and risk I've incurred bringing you here to share the final cut.

As you'd see if your sockets held more than the slick, papery remnants of your putrefied green eyes, the lost footage isn't grainy or difficult to view. Every frame is clear. I'm a professional, not a hack. Every action takes place in good light, photographed from accessible angles, without disruptive jumpy edits or glitches in the stock. Nevertheless, what we see on the infamous lost footage remains inexplicable.

The boys become like twelve-year-old children. They

may be bullies, but they are afraid. Their souls corrupt before the tip of my tongue touches their invisible anxiety. Love kills everything. It's all one big fuck, man. That's what the king said. Nothing ever needs to make sense again.

The sound of a church makes the boys shiver. Off camera, the eyes of an exorcist peel apart layers of anatomy like diagrams from an old encyclopedia. I look to the left and a nuclear reaction asks silver of their skin. Glowing, the boys untangle like the woven reams beneath the hard shell of a golf ball or like the strings of snot streaming from the nostrils of infected swine. I gesture, and the boys spin in a carousel of altered grime.

On camera they appear striated, as if run through an industrial peeler and pinned into thin strips prepped by bloodless miscreants licking sticky fingers. The boys are shiny with desire. Deconstructed, they sizzle on the tongues of the reprobate workers, stinging the many paper cuts in the diligent fetishist's moist fervent mouths.

A bloodless vivisection and weaving of venous matter decorates the screen. What substance the boys possessed as autonomous beings has mutated into a food for me, a plum toned gel that I vomit onto their torsos after eating between the spaces where the threads of flayed and intertwined flesh suggest extraterrestrial original forms. Odors of unknown worlds pollute the static frames of the film, and we viewers of the lost footage remain haunted by the sickly rising smell of an alien's massacred cunt. The boys and their assailants are forgotten tampons in her maw.

Heaving together, for they are twined into a long fleshy cord, the boys resemble saplings twisted into a single trunk, striving for light. Their bark is skin and their limbs quiver in pain. Without woody resilience they sag most pink and pathetically.

I have done all I can to give them new life. Life is foolish.

It seeks death no matter what one offers. No matter how hard one tries.

In one previous life, I worked on a farm. I labored in the earth's rich humus and thought only of the next dig, the next harvest, and the coming fall. I followed seasons as they changed. I slept heavily and well.

One day I dug too deep and met a strange animal that entered my navel and asked how many deaths I wanted to eat.

All of them, I said.

Since then, my answer is always yes.

So the boys on film crawl out of their confines as if each separate organ and anatomical system despises the rest. Nerve endings whip and curl into knots. Muscle pulses against crackling silver skin as lungs blast open to fracture ribs. Hearts spurt lush streams of blood upward, aimed to blind. The strange cone of coagulate created by the boys, cleaned by the miscreants, and discarded by goddesses intent on flowery foolish concourse with eternity slumps down to the pit we reside in. Slumps down before me like a last meal, where all matter ends.

This is my purpose, I suppose, in the vast toilet of the cosmos. To love what whirls away unloved. To embrace the waste of careless demiurges cast out by life and death and the lunacy of terrible kings. To love what is lost.

And in the famous lost footage, the piles of meat that were once the misbehaving boys quake, grow wings, and take flight. Their owl-like voices resound throughout the forest, leading us astray. We wander agape as we seek the familiarity of the city and the disco where you will fall to your death later that night.

~

KEEP HOLDING MY HAND, John. I promise this won't hurt.

Yes, darling, you're right. I'm lying. It's going to hurt a lot.

We're lost among the ruins, a consequence of damaging the dancing boys. I've never claimed to be subtle, have I?

Tricksters call from the depths of a directionless world. Voices hoot and echo. Perilous in the woods, cajoling unseen from afar, puzzling our sense of direction through descending darkness and the repetition of leaves, bark, and mosses, their comely voices call.

I pull back the sheet draped over your cold body in my wish-fulfilling memory. Here, do you see? The glow of shadow impassioned in a close crimp is evidence of your hidden life. Something in you still burns. You have to fold time quite intensely to see it, cut out all the bad parts. The love that lies here holds still in jest. My love is the love that whirls.

But I didn't pull back the sheet, did I?

I turned away.

∾

LOST AMONG THE RUINS, John has enacted the golden sacrifice. He danced badly in his role. He knows it. He needs a drink.

He yells. I'm so sick of the way he yells.

On and on, his complaints. "You stupid cunt, why did you have to kill them? We'll die out here for fuck's sake."

His breathing isn't right. He sniffs violently as if I can be tricked into thinking he's a tough guy instead of a whining bore. My lovely boy has grown to be a great needy burden. Furthermore, we haven't fucked in ages.

"Don't be such a child," I say.

He balks and gasps and then punches a tree trunk and swerves around on me. "Oh, I'm a child now? Well, fuck me. All this time I thought that's exactly what you were after."

I have nothing to say in my defense. "This may come as a

shock to you, darling, but yes, I do happen to prefer younger men."

John flounders in panic. Spit flies from his lips. "You're a fucking pervert. You're a *thing*. I don't even know what you are. I want to go home. I don't need any of this."

"You're right. You don't need me. Whatever was I thinking taking care of you all this time?

The hurt bleeds from his pupils.

"Fuck you," John says, flinging tears. "Get someone else to wipe your ass and plough your dried up old twat."

I pretend to laugh, looking through the treetops at the unwelcoming night sky. "Well. I see somebody's buzz is wearing off. Too bad baby's eaten up all the acid Daddy fed them and the nearest cocktail lounge is miles and miles away."

His fist shocks me once and then shocks me again.

John curses as I hit the ground. I tumble and he keeps yelling. He barrels away into the woods. According to the star Polaris by which I can navigate in the night, he's going the wrong direction to reach the city. He'll be lost indefinitely. He won't make it to the club tonight. He keeps on cursing at me as he recedes, but I can't hear what he says any longer.

It's all going dark. Numb.

In this version, my final edit of the film, I don't call him back or get up and go after him.

I lie in the moss unfolding as John exits with my heart. All that's left is a paper cut.

Maybe he'll live and have a normal chance at love, at maturity and family, at the mundane pleasures of a less indulgent life. Maybe he'll be stronger if all his wishes aren't granted. He'll feel like he's missing out, but maybe he'll get back all the time I've taken from him. John will never understand how he called me forth and formed me, how his was the power to unmake the monster he wrought. *Damn you,* he'll say, and I'll take it. Whatever curse he offers. I'll fade into nothing but a bad dream, an unpleasant memory of an old creep who picked him up when he was foolish and young.

As the years pass, he'll wonder how much of it he made up.

"All of it," I say to no one as a whirl of dislodged leaves cascades down to trade out corpses and bury my desiccated face.

CRUMBS

JOSHUA R. PANGBORN

"*O*pen that hole. *Wider*."

My eyes bulge as I struggle to obey.

"Watch the teeth. How are the cuffs?" His gritty hand smacks my face, drawing tears. "Don't speak."

"But how can I—"

His hand slides along moist lips as it presses tightly over my open mouth. "*Don't. Speak*."

I nod. My nose is dripping snot. He removes his hand, wiping it on my hair.

"Now. Cuffs. Tight enough?"

I jerk my arms, cowhide biting into dough.

"Good. Good Fatboy." He rubs my check with the back of his hand, whatever had dried on there flaking off in the process. "I'm puttin' it in your mouth, now. Don't do anything. Just let it sit there for a minute. Let it roll 'round on your tongue."

He glides it in, slowly, teasingly. Taunting me.

"That's it. That's a good Fatboy. Feel it in there. Taste it. Imagine that cream sliding down your throat."

I grunt to breathe.

"Now. Go ahead and chew it."

The soggy Oreo is reduced to crumbs in seconds.

"That's it, Fatboy. Now swallow." I love when he calls me that, 'Fatboy.' His teasing just makes me hungrier. Hornier. Happier. All those words starting with H.

He's straddling me, riding the waves of my stomach.

"Another. Take another."

He moans a little as I chew. His tongue traces the curve of my stomach.

"Open."

He shoves in another before I'm done with the second and leans his flushed face towards me.

"That's it, Fatboy. Eat." He's breathing heavier now, so full of pride and awe.

Then he dies.

I WAKE up in the same room I went to sleep in. Which, when you think about it, is how it's supposed to be. I don't remember falling asleep. Though I suppose that, too, is normal.

The lamp by the bed is still on from last night. Clothes are piled on the floor by the door, which is shut. Force of habit, even though we don't have to worry about privacy. From when I was a kid. My mother was always shouting at me:

Ray, we don't live in a barn, shut your door.

Ray, your TV's too loud, shut your door.

Ray, if you really need to jerk off, shut your door.

My briefs, worn in the seat, fabric stretched everywhere but the pouch, had somehow landed on the computer monitor last night. There's the corner of a message box on the computer screen behind the briefs. Someone had sent a note. Maybe for me. Probably for me. Jeremiah hates the computer.

I stare up at the ceiling. Water stain from the floor above.

Keeps growing. I just know one day we're going to wake up in sludge.

What'll I have for lunch today? There's still a pizza left, I only got down two of them last night. Will that be enough? No. Probably should warm up that pie I got at the bakery yesterday too. *But what about dinner?*

I look down at Jeremiah, lying on my chest. He's still dead, of course. He won't be much help deciding what to eat today. Which kind of sucks because that's sort of his responsibility. His face is still buried between my tits. As my mother always said: *If they bounce when you run, Ray, they're tits, don't matter if you've got a cock or not.*

My arms are a bit numb. I'd tried tugging and pulling to get them out of the cuffs. That hurt. Didn't work, obviously, otherwise I probably would have called an ambulance by now. But these cuffs are pretty strong and the keys are on the shelf by the window. No help over there.

So. Dinner. I could throw together some pasta. I think there are a few boxes of medium shells in the cupboard. But I'm not a big fan of pasta. Jeremiah is always pushing me to eat it because pasta's so high in calories, but I can never really stomach more than a box, box and a half. Then he gets mad. Still, if I'm only having one pizza for lunch, I'll be hungry enough, probably…

Jeremiah is getting a bit heavy.

"Fat lot of good you are. You're supposed to be making all these tough decisions," I say to his head. He doesn't answer, but I do see that he's got a bald spot. Strange I'd never noticed this.

"All right, if you're just going to lie there, I'll have to do something about this." I start to thrust my hips up and down, gyrating against his lower half. I curl my toes around purple cotton sheets and plunge harder, faster, faster, harder. He bounces a little and his head comes off my chest for an instant. I hold my breath and continue to gather my momentum, *harder faster faster harder.*

Finally, I thrust upwards with my hips at an angle. It's enough to drive Jeremiah's body into the air. It bounces onto the mattress next to me and continues to bounce onto the floor with a wet papier-mâché sound. I lick my dry lips. Somehow I had bitten my cheek, so I suck the blood until I have a mouthful and swallow. I start to breathe again and my chest is rising up and down in fast, shallow gulps.

I have a hard-on.

I haven't seen my penis for three years. It's still there, of course. I mean, I can feel the piss running down my leg in the shower. And every time Jeremiah's on top of my belly, naked, with food, it'll make itself known. Sometimes it doesn't take food, though. Like right now. So, I'm intact. Really. I just haven't *seen* it. Sort of just a big opening surrounded by fat. Sometimes I catch Jeremiah gazing in admiration as I'm doing chores—my near nullification a thing of beauty to him.

A scuttling from under the bed tries to distract me from my erection. But, I tug on the cuffs again, even though I know they'll hold, stubborn. Like the animal they're made from. No, those are mules. Cows aren't stubborn, but they are *delicious.* The cuffs still hold and I'm still stuck. I really want to wrap my hand around it right now.

"This is pathetic."

I nod my head in agreement.

"I mean, really, look at you. You can't even take care of your own dick without my help."

My eyes tingle as sweat drips down my forehead and into them.

"Who's there?"

I hear a laugh. Deep, masculine. Empty.

"Fatboy, have you forgotten 'bout me already?" The voice is coming from the floor, by the bed.

"Jeremiah? What are you doing on the floor?"

Ten fingers worm up the edge of the bed. They dig into the purple cotton and Jeremiah's head rises from below.

"You knocked me on the floor, Fatboy."

"Yeah, but you were dead then."

He's pulled himself into a sitting position on the edge of the bed. One of his fingers starts swirling around my nipple.

"Still am."

"That sucks. Can I have another Oreo?"

He stops circling my nipple. "Nope. Not gonna happen, Fatboy."

I stick out my bottom lip and scrunch up my eyes. "But I'm so hungry."

"Do you think you deserve one? I mean, you did throw my body to the floor."

That wasn't very nice of me. "That wasn't very nice of me."

He shakes his head. I laugh. When he stops shaking his head, his eyes keep spinning around, only the left one doesn't quite make it all the way and so it's backwards now. There's only white there. And it's glowing.

JEREMIAH'S still sitting next to me when I come back. He's pointing at something, a big smile on his face. I look down. There's an eyeball in my bellybutton and it blinks. "Why won't you feed me?" my stomach gurgles in a high-pitched whine. The tiny bellybutton eye starts to cry milky tears and my whole belly shakes. "I'm so hungry, Ray. You have no idea. Please, give me something to eat."

I want to reach down and pet it, tell it everything will be okay. Jeremiah used to stroke it, but I know he won't caress it again even if I ask him to. And I can see him shaking his head. He knows what I want him to do. His eyes still keep spinning when his head stops, so I can't help but laugh again.

"It's not nice to laugh at me, Fatboy."

Unused stomach acid has worked its way up the back of my throat while I was out. I swallow it back down, tasting the burn. "Sorry, Jeremiah."

He slaps me across the face. "Don't do it again, Fatboy." He jumps out of bed. "Damn, Fatboy, this place is disgusting. These pizza boxes are from three weeks ago. Damn! You don't got to do much around here. All you got to do is what I ask, and I pay for everything." He turns to me. His face is purple like the sheets.

"Jeremiah…can…can you feed me something? I'm awful hungry."

He smirks and one of his teeth falls out. He picks it up and sets it on the shelf by the keys. The sun reflects off it.

Jeremiah walks across the room to the phone by the computer, putting his hand on the receiver. I blink and it's in his hand, and he's about to dial. Then he sees me staring at him, and he winks before sliding it back into the cradle. He always does this after he ties me up, likes to pretend he's going to leave me this way.

"I wish you wouldn't," I'd said to him before. He laughed those times, too. I'd tried to tell him about Freddie, with his big, mean eyes and rough hands, how he'd tie me up naked in the showers at gym class and leave me for the teacher to find.

"You can't leave me," I'd beg Freddie.

"Sucks to be you," he'd say, turning the cold water on.

He's just jealous of you, Ray. All those little fuckers at school'll regret not being nicer to you, 'cause you're gonna be somebody!

But Jeremiah only laughed about Freddie. He'd slammed his fist into my gut, which was way smaller then, and told me how much he knew I probably loved what Freddie did to me. That's what Freddie had said too, his hand on my boner in that shower stall. Then he shoved his own in my mouth and threatened me with a beating if he felt teeth. After, as I dripped dry, shivering, he ran his hands over goose-pimpled flesh, pulling me close. Then he kissed me through tears of his own. We dated for most of high school, until Freddie died in a car accident.

"You're a natural sub, how else'd you explain ending up as my pig," Jeremiah had said, hitting me again. Then he licked my cheek and shoved half a Milky Way in my mouth.

He got his jollies off watching other guys get fat. Now tell me, what was I to make of that? I mean, mothers warn you about guys who will take advantage of you for money, who will use you for sex and then dump you flat—*I don't mind you're gay, Ray, but I'm just worried about AIDS and people beating you up*—but never once do mothers tell you what to do when the guy you're dating wants to double your ass size.

Jeremiah's circling the room. "Please let me go. I'm just so hungry." He's staring at the computer now. The briefs are still covering the screen.

"Don't think I realized just how big you've gotten. These things cover the whole screen."

"You did this to me, Jeremiah. You shouldn't be surprised by how big they are—you kept encouraging me along."

More deep laughter. "I didn't do anything you didn't ask me to."

The bellybutton eye is still crying. It's getting dark out and shadows make funny shapes on Jeremiah's purple skin. The one eye of his, still backwards. He's right, of course. When I saw how hot it got him after that first feeding, how hard it got him, I'd asked him to keep doing it. I'd even signed the contract to prove how much I wanted him to do it. That first night, I must have finished off two pizzas then, and that was a lot for me three years ago. But the way he looked at me, I could see the glowing in his eyes. As he slowly brought that first piece of pizza to my lips and told me to chew, he was fighting back the biggest smile. He rubbed my bloated belly after the first eight slices were gone, and he couldn't stop that little shudder from escaping. He'd even leaked a little from his cock, and he massaged it in with the sweat on my belly. I must have been feeling the same feelings he was, but all I can remember is him.

"Why won't you let me go?" I plead with him.

He walks to the pile of clothes by the door. He kicks aside my size 46s to get to his own jeans underneath. He pulls out a wrinkled square from one of his pockets, tossing the jeans back into the mess. He unfolds it slowly, using just the tips of his dirty, grimy fingers. Three years I've lived with him. Belonged to him is a better way to say it. And this paper is why.

"Five years, Fatboy. You agreed to be my slave for five-*fucking*-years. And you asked me for this. This is all you." He holds the unfolded paper in front of me, pointing to the signatures with a muscular finger. "See?" He rubs the paper in my face. "See?"

I nod my head up and down. Three years, three amazing years of food, and sex, and his approving—even loving—smile. I hadn't realized how I'd let him corrupt me, transform me into something pathetic, servile. My mother recognized it though, the moment she saw me after three years apart. Her face fell, and she pointed out all the things that were wrong with me, with my life, with my body. *You're letting it happen again, Ray. You're letting a no-good loser pull you down and squander your potential, just like that Freddie tried to do in high school.*

Jeremiah pulls the paper away, folding it up again, and I notice that one of his fingers has fallen off and is still on my face. Meat is meat, so I wriggle my tongue, licking the tip of it, but I can't get it closer to bite. I suck in my cheek between my teeth to create a slope, but it does no good. The finger is not budging. Jeremiah slaps it away and it smacks against something I can't see with a wet thud.

I turn my head and vomit a little of the stomach acid that has made its way back into my throat. My gut clenches tightly, and the screams it is screaming must surely be loud enough for the neighbors to hear. They will come and help save me from Jeremiah. No one comes, of course. They never do. My three eyes are all crying now. Purple Jeremiah is sitting next to me on the bed again.

"No good crying, Fatboy. You know that. Just sit back and take what you have coming to you."

I lick my lip again, drinking snot and tears. He really isn't going to feed me. Or free me. "You're supposed to be dead," I say.

"I am. I told you that."

"But why'd you have to go and die before you'd untied me?"

He shrugs. He grabs one of his arms and tears it off so I can see inside the hole, all the strings and tubes that make up the body.

"Bet this would be real tasty, wouldn't it?"

I nod, and my breathing gets faster.

"Jesus, someone likes what they see," he says, poking my sudden erection with the arm. Then he tosses the arm into a corner. "Thought you were real smart, eh, Fatboy? Thought you could pull a fast one on ol' Jeremiah, didn't you? Them fancy brains of yours aren't much help now, though, eh?"

"I didn't mean to." The rolling pin had felt light in my hands, though. And the pills weren't that solid. It had really been so easy to grind them up every night and put them in his beer. And as long as it wasn't his first beer of the night, he couldn't taste them.

"Yeah, well you did it anyway. But what a fucking geek way to kill someone! Overdosing them on *pat-asseum*?"

"Potassium."

He slaps me again. "Don't fucking correct me, Fatboy. It's *pat-asseum* if I says it is. And it's a damn faggoty way of killing someone. Hyperkalemia? Shit, Fatboy."

"I just wanted out. I didn't know what else to do!"

He looks at me. Then he breaks off one of the fingers on his remaining hand and jabs it into the bellybutton eye. I scream out of sympathy. The shards of white bone are left sticking out of it, blood and pus dripping down the waves of my belly. Jeremiah's getting dressed as I watch the blood ooze.

"Well, now, seems to me you done made your bed, it's best you lie in it, Fatboy. You wanted your freedom, you got it."

He's opening the door to the bedroom, kicking aside my clothes. The right sleeve of his shirt dangles, empty.

"Wait, where are you going? You have to help me."

He shakes his head. The right eye is now facing backwards, too, when the spinning stops. "Don't gotta do nuthin'. Thought you could take care of yourself, Fatboy, but you didn't think it through."

"I didn't know it would kill you when I was tied up!"

He shrugs his left shoulder, his right one having nothing left to shrug. He shuts the door on his way out. Then I hear his voice, from the other side.

"Sucks to be you, don't it?"

Then even his voice was gone, and I am left alone. Free. I tug again at my restraints, feeling the edges slice into my wrists like a knife through butter. My arms, wet with sweat and blood, twitch even after I have given up, refusing to quit. Because I'm not a quitter. I always find a way out, a way to escape those holding me back. I was able to break free from Freddie. And now Jeremiah. I have so much potential ahead of me now.

Free. I am free. I am...

I am *hungry.*

THREE FOR A FUNERAL

K.S. WALKER

he night has never been as quiet as this—the crickets are silent, the freeway in the distance muted. It's all narrowed down to this girl in my arms and even though it's full dark no moon I can see her heart beat a staccato pulse in the side of her neck. It's the only sight, the only sound that is important to me. I lick my lips around these new teeth swelling from my gums. Magic trips along my ribcage, buzzes in my lungs. It is borrowed. I have claimed this magic with Diana's help, but life is cruel and it has not yet claimed me back. Her mouth is covered in blood that isn't hers and her lips are mouthing words for me and me alone.

"Please. Please, remember," she begs on whispered breath. And for a moment, I do.

It was not supposed to happen like this.

It's a Saturday afternoon and my cell phone buzzes in my back pocket. The bakery is slow, and really there's only one person who would bother calling me. I make eyes at the new kid to cover the register, and step into the back near the deep freezer.

"Yeah?"

"Come over. I got something for you to see. Wait a sec— Granny! Can Ashley come over?"

"I didn't even say yes yet," I laughed. It doesn't matter much though. Diana's home is my second home. Wait. "Which granny?"

She laughs, a shiny thing. "Aw, you know. Granny Maeve."

Which is a good thing because me and her Nish granny are cool, but her Black granny still doesn't like me. She caught us kissing in the sixth grade back when Diana's bedroom was the color of a sunrise and before she painted the walls a blue so dark it looks black in most light. She thinks I made Diana gay. Never mind that Diana dates dudes most of the time, or that she kissed me first or that, well, for me? It's complicated.

"I get off at three. I'll be over then."

"What's that?" Diana is yelling into her house again. "Granny says bring her a chocolate muffin."

At 3:25 I'm parking my Ford Taurus in Diana's driveway. It's a long one-story brick ranch with a walkout basement and baskets of petunias along the porch. Diana's mom is an ER nurse and works long hours. She usually has one of Diana's grandma's over to—I don't know— *watch her*? Diana says her mom's got trust issues, only it's not Diana she doesn't trust. It's the world. She doesn't have to explain it to me though. I remember Tommy and how things changed after he went away. Granny Maeve is always saying how the trouble with Tommy is he was always messing around with things that didn't concern him. And why go looking for trouble? He's big and Black and Indian. Trouble's always gonna find him

on its own. We'll be for real grown by the time Tommy gets out.

I walk in the front door and set a bakery box of muffins on the counter, two chocolate and two blueberry.

"Hi, Granny Maeve!" I call out so that she can hear me over the sound of the game show she's watching.

"Ashley! *Aaniin!*" Granny Maeve calls back to me as she raises herself from an armchair. "What are you two up to this afternoon?"

Diana appears out of the hallway. She's wearing an oversized sweatshirt that it's much too hot for. I'm not surprised —she still hasn't told anyone. Well, no one except for the kid's dad.

Me, I was there when she peed on that damn stick. I held her hand as we watched a little plus sign appear like a reverse magic trick. She took three more pregnancy tests before it sunk in. Then she crumpled against me as if I were hollow and she could crawl inside for safety. It was the softest I'd ever seen Diana. And I'll be honest, it scared the shit out of me.

She grabs a muffin from the box and tugs at my elbow. "Homework, Granny! We gotta go," Diana says, hustling me out of the kitchen.

"C'mon. I figured it out," she whispers to me.

This? This is the Diana I know. And *it?*

That would be her plan for retribution.

WE GO TOGETHER, see? Since we were nine years old it's been Diana and Ash, Ash and Diana. Things were simpler then, before boobs and first periods. When things got complicated we still rode just as hard for each other.

In the eighth grade I got tired of watching Rick Turner pull her ponytails and asking if he could be her John Smith. I punched him in the back of his head and he hasn't done it since.

In the tenth grade I walked into a party just as Brady Mitchell was telling everyone I'd be at least a nine if my hair wasn't so nappy. Diana poured her beer over his head and marched over to me. She grabbed me by the waist and pulled me flush against her. We never talk about it, but I think she knows I wasn't into that kiss either. But she was doing it for show, so I guess it was okay. I should probably tell her I'm not trying to be kissed by anybody.

So when she showed up at my front door one evening with a busted lip and eyes hard and shiny like volcanic glass and told me Kyle's out of the picture, I nodded and said okay. I knew what was supposed to come next.

DIANA USHERS me into her bedroom and clicks the door shut behind us. It's not navy black anymore, these days Diana's room is a rich purple flecked with gold. Something royal. I collapse onto her bed and wait for the reveal. Diana is nothing if not a showman. Except the flourish never comes.

Instead she's on hands and knees digging through her closet which is barely contained chaos on the best of days. Today the barriers have slipped and pair-less shoes, shredded denim, scraps of underwear are spilling forth, unfurled like a tongue. At last she stands and she's holding something she's wrapped in a black satin cloth.

She sits on the bed and sets the bundle between us.

"I found it at Granny Deb's house. In her library."

I haven't seen it since middle school, but I remember it well. Diana's Granny Deb has this little room off the kitchen. Floor to ceiling shelves built right into the walls. In the center of the room there was a low-back loveseat, a short round table with a reading lamp. I never did like reading as much as Diana. But I did enjoy the hushed mystery of exploring that room, and the ritual of sitting shoulder to shoulder with Diana as she read aloud.

Diana pulls the satin away revealing a journal-sized book with a soft brown leather cover. There are symbols that remind me of the zodiac embossed in the leather, and I drag my fingertips across them. The book is humming with energy.

So here's the thing about me—I'm not superstitious or nothing, but I'm not dumb either. My Mom always burned the hair she pulled clean from brushes and combs or after a trim. She told me she does it because her mom taught her to. I asked my grandma about it once, and she says she does it because it's the way *her* mother taught her to. But not only that, otherwise birds make a nest of your hair and it'll turn you crazy. Listen. I don't think the sparrows and pigeons in my neighborhood got it like that. But I do know that when I'm sitting next to her and she's burning clumps of black coily hair, I can *feel* it. Like a tautness in the air begging to be released and doesn't let up until the last of it is choking smoke. So yeah, I burn the hair that comes loose after a good detangling. It doesn't have anything to do with the birds though, and everything to do with power. And this book, sitting on Diana's constellation-patterned comforter? It has power.

Curiosity gets the better of me. I pull the book onto my lap and flip through it. It's not unlike flipping through my grandmother's rolodex of recipe cards. These pages are bound copies of someone's narrow, angular handwriting. There's lists, drawings, numbered procedures. And that's when it hits me. I snap the book shut and all but fling it towards Diana.

"That's a spell book!"

Diana is looking at me. She's chewing her lip and her eyes are wide, expectant.

"You think it's real?" There's an eagerness in Diana's voice that I've never heard before. So here's the other thing: Diana's not dumb either. And more than that, she's *spiritual*. It's been almost a decade since she chewed me out for conflating her daddy's side's, her Anishinaabe side's, medicine with magic—I haven't forgotten. But she *believes* in both. I know she feels whatever I feel thrumming through that book, so I don't even answer that.

As much as I want to say 'This is crazy!' or 'Fuck it I'm out,' I don't. Even though every hair on my arm is standing on end, I want to know what's in this book. What's in it that calls to me so strongly, creeping up my fingertips and across my skin?

"What are you gonna do?" I ask.

Diana slides close to me, until we're shoulder-to-shoulder, flipping through a book like we used to. Except the book is in my lap this time, and she's just looking over my shoulder. There's a truth serum, a love potion, a fertility curse and a vitality blessing. I see ingredients like willow root, chamomile, moon water and crow feathers. There's pages with one word spells, there's pages filled to the edges with cramped writing, words scratched out and re-written. Orishas are named next to the Lords of Xibalbá. I don't think this book belongs to any one religion, not to any one group of people, but instead it's someone's collection of Old World tales and tonics expanded and blended into something new. *This is diaspora magic.* Scattered but not forgotten. New blossoms, same roots. I find the page that Diana has in mind; I know it without her saying a single thing.

I stroke my thumb across the creature drawn in the upper right hand corner and my mouth goes dry.

"We do the spell. Give Kyle a scare or two. Teach him a lesson and maybe he won't be such a dickhead to the next girl..." she trails off.

"But?"

"It's just, with the baby. It doesn't say anything about changing with a baby."

"I get it," I tell her. It takes two tries to pry the words from my parched throat, but it's true. I do get it. She may be scared as hell to tell her family, but I know how much she loves that kid already.

"But for you, it should be safe. Then we do the healing spell before the sun rises and you should be back to normal."

Should be. Those words rouse me.

"What if it doesn't work? How do we know any of it works?"

I follow Diana's gaze across the room. There's a terrarium taking up the entire top of her dresser and I can't believe I didn't notice it there before. In it are origami cranes, giving the impression of having been hastily folded. At least two are made from soft college-rule. Some are still. Others flutter-hop around each other. There's no mistaking it, they are all alive.

She takes the book from my lap and flips a few pages then hands it back to me. She points to the title: Minor Animations.

"What counts as a Major Animation?"

"I asked the same thing," she says as she flips two more pages. In the margins is written: *Mammals preferred. Best if the intended sacrifice is at least half the weight of the corpse you intended to revive.*

I shut the book; I don't need to read anymore. Instead, I go to get a closer look at the flock that Diana has created. With my nose pressed against the glass I can see lines where the paper has gone soft, from Diana's folding or wear on their own bodies I can't tell.

"What do I need to do?" I ask without turning away from the glass. I can hear Diana ruffle the pages.

"Mostly be a willing participant." She's holding up the page with the creature again. It looks like a cross between a bear and a bat, and I wish I could laugh at it but its misproportioned body turns my stomach. The arms are too spindly, too long. The jaw too loose. The knees might be backwards, but I don't want to look close enough again to tell. "Consent is underlined three times here. The rest...the rest is kind of easy. I'll need to grab a few things. It only works under the right conditions. Needs to be a new moon, for one."

"When's the next one?" I ask turning to face her. Diana looks up at me. She has already done this math, and I don't know if I should be impressed at her thoroughness or pissed at her for making assumptions.

"Three days from now." So I have three days to decide if I want to go through with this. I'll never say it out loud, but there's a small part of me that is thrilled by the prospect; to put on a monster's skin, wield all the power and damn the consequences. And that small voice? It scares the hell out of me. But this is Diana I'm talking about. She's never asked me for a damn thing she didn't need. And besides, has there ever been anything I wouldn't do for her?

~

DIANA OUTLINES THE SUPPLIES, the steps with clinical efficiency, but it does nothing to mask her simmering excitement. When she finishes I stand up and tell her, "Let me think about it."

Diana nods. "It'll take me a day or two to get everything we'll need."

"I'll let you know by tomorrow."

Then Diana takes me into one of her bone crushing hugs. I feel the tight swell of Diana's baby pressing into my own belly. It's firmer than I expected.

The drive home is one of those drives that feels like an out-of-body experience. My hands guide me down familiar streets, my eyes seeing—but not really—and the next thing I know I'm parked outside my house. The driveway is empty, but I never pull in. I let my dad use the driveway so it's a shorter walk inside. He'd never admit it, but I think his hip is getting worse.

Dad's worked night shifts as long as I can remember, and he always leaves me a note before he goes. It used to be in a lunch box for me to find at school the next day. Today he's left a note on the kitchen counter saying that there's lasagna in the fridge: *Preheat the oven to 400°. Cook for one hour.* Signed with three hearts. I put the lasagna in the oven and pour myself a bowl of cereal.

Before the oven chimes I know what I will tell Diana.

WHEN MY DAD was nineteen he totaled his Chevy Impala with his best friend in the passenger seat. A last minute decision behind the wheel saved his friend's life and ruined my Dad's left leg. They pinned my Dad's hip back together and Uncle Dave came over every other Sunday for dinner with us. Until one time Uncle Dave left and mom left with him.

Dad goes through every day with screws in his hip and a knife in his back, and he's still probably the most thoughtful and patient person I know. I asked him once if he regretted that split-second choice. He looked me in the face with his lips pressed into a fierce line and a furrow to his brow. "Never," he said. "Not even once."

There's a business card on the fridge for the specialist he has a referral to see about a total hip replacement. The card has gone yellow from the sun.

I don't call or text Diana the next day. I skip school Monday. On Tuesday after school I find her leaning on the hood of my car.

"Let's do it," I say. My smile feels watery. But if it looks shaky she doesn't mention it. She just smiles.

"You're the best, Ash."

The praise settles warmly in my chest. "Where next?"

She rummages through her bag a second and her hand emerges holding a small re-purposed jam jar.

"Drink this." Turns out Diana has been busy with or without my answer. But she knows me. Knows me best.

If Diana told me this was creek water I wouldn't be surprised--brownish specks are suspended in an off-yellow liquid. Some of the particles are already starting to fall to the bottom. She frowns then gives the jar a hard shake and cracks the lid. Diana leans forward and sniffs it before grinning brightly and extending the jar to me. It smells citrusy and warm, like the burst of fragrance from the black walnuts that cover Diana's yard. I'm not sure if the chill snaking its way up my spine is a warning or excitement but before I can consider or change my mind I take the jar from Diana and swallow it down in three long drinks.

Whatever she gave me is cool and more viscous traveling down my throat than it felt sliding past my tongue. The residue left on my lips is sticky and acerbic. I wipe my hand across the back of my sleeve.

"And now we wait," Diana says, rocking back on her heels. "Pick me up at eight?"

"And Kyle? What about him?"

"I've got that covered. Just pick me up at eight, yeah?"

My stomach is a tangle of nervous excitement, the promise of power trembling through me. If this works...*damn!* Things are never going to be the same for either of us again.

~

I PARK in Diana's driveway at eight exactly. Even more surprising, Diana is waiting for me. Neither of us have been this on time in our lives. She's sitting on the front step and there are two backpacks beside her. Diana flashes me a smile and I toss her my keys. My hands are shaking too much to drive, and besides, she knows where we're going.

Soon we're outside of the city. The windows are down and energy crackles between us, as if the very night knows what we are going to attempt to do and is urging us forward. Diana takes the next turn too fast. I brace my hands on the dash and root my feet to the floor and try to melt into the turn. She is lightning, and I am the cloud that carries her. Diana trills into the night. For the first time since she taught me, when we were in overalls and training bras, I trill back.

We pull up at a public access entrance for Reed's Lake. I look at Diana.

"We used to come out here to watch the stars fall," she says without looking back.

There is a space of silence between us. I know what it's like to feel discarded. But there are threads of a different sort of heartsickness embroidered in her pain. She shakes off the memories of her and Kyle and it's all electric business again.

"Let's get you ready."

I follow Diana down a path of crushed grass until we're out of view of where she parked the car. They say hurt people, hurt people. And I know Diana's hurt goes deeper than that busted lip Kyle gave her. He's a shitbag for the way he treated her after knocking her up, but I still wonder how far this is meant to go. It's all in Diana's hands now though. She gives me four palm-sized rocks, only distinguishable to me by texture in this darkness. She instructs me to place them as if I were making an X and to stand in their center.

From the other backpack she pulls out a large mason jar full of a dark liquid. For the first time I feel doubtful.

"I don't have to drink that too, do I?" Shame on me for not reading the fine print.

"No, but I do need a drop of your blood." I laugh at first, but then I make out the smoothness of Diana's face. She's serious. "Only, like, *a drop* though." She produces a safety pin.

I hold my hand out to her, but she shakes her head. "You have to do it. Remember that whole willing and consent thing?"

I shove the safety pin into my pointer finger and squeeze until I coax two droplets forward.

"I love you, Ashley. You really are the best." I can feel her smile even in the dark.

Diana brings the jar up to her mouth and whispers words she must have memorized. I don't hear them, but they sound soothing, like the tone you'd use to hush a baby back to sleep. Then she spreads the liquid around me in a circle, connecting the rocks I've laid. She begins with the one in front of me. A flash of headlights shine through the trees in the distance. Kyle must have arrived; Diana works faster.

The spot where she has poured her trail begins to sizzle with cold smoke that drifts straight upward rather than wherever it pleases. Diana completes her circle and steps back to admire her work. She gives me one last smile through this swirling column I am ensconced in, then heads back towards the dirt parking lot to do whatever she has planned to do to get Kyle out here.

The only direction I can see clearly in is up. I tilt my head to take in the starry night; The new moon is heavy in its absence. I can feel it like bated breath. And that's when it begins—my lungs spark like there's been a match lit behind my diaphragm. Each breath in drags sandpaper down my trachea. There is a searing pain that ricochets from my elbows through the pads of each of my fingers. My shoulders bulge and shift, the sound of them dislocating and relocating bringing wave after wave of nausea. The fibrous things that hold me together are becoming undone. I am becoming remade. And though I am standing I can feel the backs of my hands brush through damp grass as my knuckles pop and contort. Spasms flash up and down my spine—it bends and bows of its own accord. There is a wrenching in my gut; My arms wrap around my body twice and I can feel my stomach torque and expand. My head is pounding and I feel like I might be split in half from skull to soles. Perhaps I have.

I don't have to wait for Diana to bring Kyle to me. The smoke column fades and I am unleashed. Voices from their direction shiver against my ears. My jaw unhinges and a long dry tongue undulates out of my mouth towards the promise of something filling. I can smell them, in my nostrils, under my tongue.

I like it.

There is a moment in which this realization fills me with revulsion, but the call is too strong, my legs tensing and twitching with the impulse to hunt.

I oblige.

I take a running start toward the lake, scamper soundlessly up a pine and then launch into the night. There is a thin membrane from thumb to torso and I don't even have to think about how to use it. I glide on an updraft. I am obscured, nightmare dark against night sky. Kyle and Diana are arguing and before he can raise his hand I land on his back claws first.

Diana yelps backward, though we tumble well away from her. It is over almost before it begins. I pull Kyle up struggling and swinging and without ceremony, I gnaw into the soft part between his jaw and his shoulder. Slick gristle works its way down my throat. There is a roaring in my ears; I am spilling more blood than I am swallowing, the urge to consume overwhelming the urge to savor, and the part of me that was disgusted is nowhere to be found. I revel in the iron tang that coats my tongue and the sticky warmth running down my chin and—

"Ash? Ashley?"

I drop Kyle. It occurs to me that she might have been calling my name for a minute now. Diana's eyes are wide, fear rolls off her in sour waves, but she doesn't tremble.

I approach her, she remains cautious but still.

"The healing spell. I have it ready already, Ash. It's in my bag. Let's go get my bag, okay? This is all okay still. You're still Ash, okay?"

This close, I am taller than Diana now. I hunch over her until my muzzle is flush with her face. Each snuff blows her hair off her forehead, her shoulder as I inhale. Flinch, after flinch. A giggle burbles out of me at the wrongness of it all. Tears form in the wells of her eyes. I can see her heart beat a staccato pulse in the side of her neck. It's the only sight, the only sound that is important to me. Her face, her mouth are covered in Kyle's blood and her lips are mouthing words for me and me alone.

"Please. Please remember, Ash."

I lick my lips around these new teeth swelling from my gums, sharp and long and throbbing. Something small inside me reminds me that she is important to me, this girl, and smaller still: *this is not how this was supposed to happen.* Blood-lust is an ache in my sternum. So I soothe it. As gentle and silent as the beating of moth wings, I slip my teeth over her heartbeat and begin to drink.

THE LAST DISGRACE

GEORGE DANIEL LEA

I chose this filthy, stinking corner of the district in vain hope that the souls drawn here might prove similarly tainted (and thereby make what I intend less terrible). I should've known better, of course. Creation has never been that kind, as others have noted when in cruel frames of mind. I invisibly fracture it where I dance, making it jagged and unclean, shards reflecting too many distorted potentials to comprehend.

If anything, those I pass, rub shoulders with, whose painted, half-lidded, lusty or drug-addled eyes I catch, are more innocent than any I've encountered in the city beyond. There's a sense of strange fraternity amongst them; of safety here. A sanctuary against the judgements of those more comfortable in their humanity, born to states of assumption and absolutism. Oh, wicked in their own peculiar ways: every brush, every breath, carrying echoes of desire, lurid intentions burning in their bellies, fantasies that have drawn them to this tainted playground.

But even the most bizarre or foetid peccadillo doesn't make them monstrous. Even those that have come lusting after the primped and painted lambs amongst the flocks, those barely beyond their high school years who ache for experience they've only known through masturbatory fantasy and internet pornography. All exude the same strange sanctity.

I don't——can't——hate them. *Any of them.* That makes it worse. Some faintly revolt me, the echoes of inclination they share eliciting shudders, nauseating in their sensory detail. But I'm used to that. The simple act of venturing beyond whatever warren I've gone to ground in elicits a cacophony of such secrets; confessions whose silent hosts wouldn't dare speak to priests or lovers. That, in many instances, they wouldn't even admit to themselves.

Here, the typical, minor frustrations and vengeance fantasies——the unbidden ruminations on raping wives into submission, beating husbands to death with claw-hammers, slaughtering employers and locking unruly or disappointing children in cellars——are absent. In their places, orgiastic tempests, fragments of drink and drug-fueled desire that lodge in my brain, slowly melting until they saturate me, one bleeding into another until I can no longer discern dreams of vengeance from sex, blood mingling with spit, sweat and semen.

Lyeman's Street, one of the first from which the city's gay district originally effloresced, is now largely forgotten to those informed by its history. An unassuming way, compared to some of the more ornamented squares, the glass and neon-fronted clubs and bars, the streets of chic boutiques and cafes that cater almost exclusively to our previously-shunned demographic. Dirtier, grimier, a place where time has crystalized everything, even the air tinted a filthy, industrial brown. The same that Victorian prostitutes and pick-pockets once breathed, those it now sustains no less predatory, albeit in a more playful vein.

I like to think that conscious inclination drew me here, the hope of finding a partner I can hate without remorse: a child abuser, a malignant narcissist, a con-artist. Maybe even another Dennis Nilsen. But no. Those who linger here remain stubbornly untainted, barring whatever petty poisons the world has cultivated in them. Little flashes of malignance, weeds that will die long, long before they have chance to flower.

It would be so easy to follow Morrow's example; abandon care, set down the confusions, the constant aching doubts, and learn to be *pure* in appetite. I envy the man, in many ways——a significant part of why I had to leave him, not that he'd ever understand. If I could only learn the trick of it, to drift through the world as though dreaming; as a dream myself. To give and take what pleasures I may before circumstance or despair conspire to snuff me out.

But it's just as the man himself said, during the escalating arguments of our latter days together:

"You ached for this. All your life, you *begged* for it. Now, you can't even let yourself *enjoy* it? It's pathetic, Sanford."

Yes. Yes, it is. *Pathetic.* To have gotten everything I wished for the escape I begged from every star and full moon. To not be part of the world, to be separate from its petty, material demands and impositions.

"Do you really hate yourself so much? How long will you punish us both for *your* regrets?"

Yes. It was best for us both that I leave. No doubt he's already found another confidante, more suited to his tastes and temperament. And I? I can lose myself in my miseries without fear of them infecting anyone else.

I catch several glances as I make my way down Lyeman's, the street flickering and misty with abstract effluent. Whilst far from as populated as the district's more fashionable environs, it still boasts its own peculiar clientele; a heady mix of older queers and younger specimens, the latter seeking some strange thrill or drawn by the oblique resonance of the place, whilst the former exude melancholia, a grey and pulsating mist that surrounds them, obscuring and distorting. Through it, I glimpse a little of what they really are, the putative states that only manifest in dreams or moments of idle, escapist fantasy. For the most part, they don't even realise, can't recall when they last brought those conditions to mind, having being shamed out of any transcendental thought many moons ago.

Regardless of age, the place tends to attract those of a like kind. Exiles from the primary tribes, non-conformists. The gay men who refute the dictates of fashion or proscribed aesthetics, coming here not in ironed or laundered outfits, but ragged jeans and ill-fitting shirts, their hairstyles shaggy and unkempt or priestly in their severity, the lesbians who conform to no cultural template of masculinity or straight man's pornography. Proscription of the sexual ideal.

Those whose eyes I snare linger on me with quiet desperation, even those that walk with lovers or domestic mates, sensing that I might relieve them of the burden they've resented since the first unasked-for mote of being kindled in their Mother's bellies.

That, at least, is a little salve. Whoever I choose, they'll thank me before the end.

MOST OF THE buildings I pass are nondescript; old Victorian structures that were once shops or small factories, mostly converted into bars and nightclubs——the former already throbbing with music, buzzing with activity, the latter awaiting the moonlit hours to throw open their doors. Punctuating them, barbers, tailors, a massage parlour. Little eateries, places to spill into following a night's intoxication, unconcerned by the quality of what grey repasts they serve. It's been an age since I've eaten anything of the sort, the grease and fat and salt, the sauce and relish. Flavours and textures I can barely recall, softened by the weight of years and less savoury meals that have occurred in between.

I know how this dance goes, one I follow reluctantly but whose steps I must complete once begun. The silent music is already so sweet, pulsing in time with the blood in my veins, urgency in the pit of my belly. Lovers call, aching for me, though they don't know it yet. Those who are outcasts even in this outcast company, that the tribe would reject for their strangeness or absurdity, their flirtation of proscribed style or accepted behaviour. They're everywhere, those lost children. I know the cracks and recesses where they make their warrens oh so well.

Lyeman's Street is a furtive and fruitful hive of such souls, its pervasive decay repelling all but the most curious and self-defined deviant. Those I pass all sing their own peculiar songs—— silently for the most part——within the drink and drug-addled cells of their heads, not even realising the laments that are plain to me: their hatred for lovers whose arms they cling to, who guide them away from sites of familiar disgrace. The sugar-daddies who are as much jailers as saviours, the cautious friends whose reason is met with slurred and sardonic contempt. One, an androgynous youth whose smile flickers in and out of being, whose half-hooded eyes betray chemical indulgences, anticipates imminent violence; the rough ropes, the uncomfortable chair, the belt that leaves weals on his back and buttocks, making him weep for want and terror of it. Another, older than his companion by a measure of decades, bemoans the child he brought into his home, one he saved from the purported abuses of parents who regarded them as tainted in their sexuality but that now treats him as little more than a surrogate father. Provider, housekeeper, cook and cleaner, their entitled temper tantrums growing more violent as the days pass.

Fodder, all. Impressions that will disperse into the earth and air unremarked, unremembered. I've seen them all, every shape of every species of every soul, from here to Sydney, from Berlin to Marrakech. Little left in all the world that might surprise me now.

~

SILENT HYMNS LEAD ME HERE, to a façade from which music of a more temporal stripe throbs——old rave tunes, for the most part, punctuated by 1990s Euphoria. My mouth waters, the plates of my skull shift. An old urge, appetites more desperate than those I scent all around rising from the dungeon below, a hunger undeniable.

Poor, lost boy, waiting somewhere in the strobe-lit dark, no shadow he can cling to, no plea or prayer he can make that will see him last the night.

Another unhappy child, another orphan despairing of its unwanted life. Despite Morrow's urgings, I can't deny my sorrow for them, each and every one. Those who regard their existence as something to be endured, silently praying, against all odds, that there will be some grander meaning, some sincere poetry, after it's done. I'm not cruel enough to tell them the futility of that vision. I'm not their Father. It isn't my business to disappoint them. I want them to die as they've never lived, for their final moments to have some of the ecstasy that's always been denied them.

This one, this grubby little run-away; one of the more pathetic, one of the more beautiful. Even were it not for his inclinations, something more fundamental to his nature would've driven him from home and hearth, kept him from any measure of comfort. Given the choice, he never would've been born in the first place.

It's almost beginning to dawn by the time I bundle the boy into the back of a taxi, whatever toxins he's happily shoveled into his system starting to take their toll. Thin threads of golden light snake through the streets, staining the dark, dank concrete, the broken and pot-holed roads.

Lyeman's is all but abandoned at this hour, save for the odd, weary soul making their sad way home from overnight jobs (or, Heaven help them, to jobs about to start). Most do everything in their power to evade us, ignore us, desperate not to snare our attentions or be drawn into unwanted discourse. That's fine. Most of them are foetid anyway, compost-souls that would disgust me were I starving for want of company.

The taxi driver knows this routine well. I scent it on him the instant we stumble into the back of the black cab, slam the door shut behind us: weary resentment, hereditary disgust that he's learned to temper over the years ferrying queer clientele to and from their debauchs.

I catch his dark, hooded eyes in the rearview mirror as we strap ourselves in, the boy laughing at nothing in particular, losing himself in a fit of delirious giggles.

"Where to, man?"

"Holden Avenue, if you please."

The man raises a bushy eyebrow, grunting affirmation. A nice estate, a decent place, he thinks. Criminal that these two faggots should have a home there. Worse than the rats in the walls, cockroaches multiplying beneath cupboards. He smells of smoke. Smoke, fire and blood. The violence in him is tantalising, making me grin as though having indulged in the same pills and powders that currently have my young friend in hysterics. An appetiser, a prophecy of the consummation to come.

"Hey, he ain't gonna puke in there, is he?"

I laugh, turning to my young friend. A subtle flex, a quiver of thought, the mildest influence. He grows silent, his head lolling as he looks up at me. The song still pulses behind his eyes, a captive dawn-bird in his skull desperate to break free.

"You aren't going to embarrass yourself like that, are you, lovely?"

He smiles, eyes fluttering, the depths of sorrow they contain almost welling, spilling down his cheeks in black trails.

"No. I promise."

"Good boy."

The driver grunts a dubious acknowledgement, content to seethe in silent fantasies of righteous violence the rest of the way.

HOLDEN AVENUE IS STILL ABED by the time we arrive. The boy steps out into the pre-dawn chill, somewhat more sober than during the trip. The driver doesn't look at me as I hand him a fifty pound note, tell him to keep the change. This close, the blood and hate is palpable, radiant, painting the air. I bathe in it, a red rain falling on my face, hearing the cries and pleas of those he considers degenerate in the eyes of God, that he prays will come to know their own loathsome-ness in the apocalypse he's dreamed of, *yearned for,* since his early adolescence. I could show him, tear open his skull and leave him naked before the abyss where god has never sat. Instead, I wish him well, thank him, let him streak away, back to his wife and children, to the home that is as much a prison as his weak and wanton flesh. A flash: legs kicking impotently at the air, the choked regrets of a man who finds no more poetry in death than he has in life. So many tomor-rows, so many miseries to come, before the final act of despair.

"Where are we?"

The boy hugs himself, shivering in the murk, casting around at the surrounding houses, all of them recessed, raised from the road on their own little mounds. Castles without kingdoms. Most dark, as though abandoned, many boasting rotting "For Rent" or "For Sale" signs, overgrown front gardens.

I draw close to him, his song scintillating, my body blossoming to it in ways he cannot perceive or appreciate yet. Such sweet despair, such dislocation. A thing cast outside of the fish bowl almost since birth, swelled to semi-manhood in the darkness beyond. He looked back in with envy, once upon a time, but has long since learned that there's nothing there for him, nothing he can love or that will love him in its turn. A dead world infested with dead people who don't understand that they've made their mortuary shuffling the measure of life itself.

"Nowhere in particular." I place an arm around his shoulders, hugging him close. He flinches at the contact, such avuncular familiarity so often either an act of quiet coercion or a prelude to cruelty.

"You...live here?"

He sounds incredulous that anyone could inhabit so Edenic a setting.

"I wouldn't say live. *Abide* might be more accurate."

He follows meek as a lamb as I lead him up the meticulously maintained garden path, away from the pre-dawn chill where all his most unwanted secrets live, happy to leave them out in the dark for once.

I don't have much requirement for heating, always happier in frosty temperatures, but I maintain a warm household for guests. The boy seats himself in front of the fire, sipping red wine. A stray brought in from the night, not knowing where to put himself or what to say.

I seat myself in the leather chair opposite, admiring him, bathing in the stories he silently confesses. So sad, almost from the very beginning. A life made broken. Never still, never fixed, never in place. A sentient splinter in the eye of creation, conscious of its nature, but unable to deny it. I drink him more earnestly than the wine, the latter lacking all but the merest traces of flavour to me——hints and echoes of those who plucked the grapes, who crushed and distilled them, who later bore the bottles to all and sundry—— whereas he is radiant and pungent and complex. A plate prepared by a craftsman, a dessert of such skill that even the old French masters would blanche.

He sits in silence, allowing me what must seem this strange moment, watching with his over-large grey and sunken eyes, not daring to speak for fear of breaking some unknown protocol.

"Did you enjoy yourself tonight?"

I know he didn't. There's no lingering trace of joy on him, no actinic qualities from the contacts he made, the vices he indulged. Just a pall of grey frustration, which, far from smothering the gold and silver inside, serves to emphasize them by contrast.

"No. I mean, there wasn't anything that interested me. Until you, that is."

I smile. "Happy to have made the night worthwhile."

He swirls wine around his glass, watching sediment settle.

"I'm not sure you have yet."

A familiar game, this coquettish dance. So often, it leads to tongues entangling in a far more literal fashion. So often, it leads to sex and sleep and the horror of a new dawn, grey and fumbling rejection. Tonight he knows better.

Standing, he comes to me in his tattered, ill-fitting jeans, his rumpled shirt, cheap jewelry tinkling at his throat, around his wrists and ankles. He seats himself in my lap, the warmth and vibrancy of him washing through me, narcotic in its potency.

The song, the song, *the song.* A bellyful of sunshine, storm-clouds in my brain. Shocks and pangs of such sincere misery, such anger and disappointment. No one, not in his entire short life, not in the days that might've come after, could ever know him, *love him* this way.

"You're a work of art. You understand that?" I smooth the unkempt, lank hair from his face, wanting to see those eyes, in all their want and confusion. He smiles.

"I've had worse pick up lines."

"I think we're a little beyond that, aren't we?"

He murmurs, mewls, curling into me, running his pale, shivering hand across my shirt, another curling around the back of my neck as he kisses my throat, the vampiric play a consistent favourite.

He saturates me. I open, blossoming invisibly, drinking him more sincerely than any imagined vampire lover. Not merely blood and spit, but his unspoken essence, echoes of memory and potential and regret that surround him. The stuff of his soul. All the days that have been or that might have been, all the decisions made and denied, the chances taken and rejected. The children he might have become, had he allowed himself. All mine, now.

A sweeter meal I can't recall, the textures of him; the shades of suicidal despair, of existential ennui, of grotesque realisations and ecstatic self-discovery, all dancing upon my palate, bloating me on vicarious experience, echoes of what can never be.

Through it all, I see him. A flickering shade, a thing of many faces, pausing to strip away its tussled shirt, revealing a scarred and bony frame, better suited to some plucked, exotic bird than a human being. A series of tattoos running down his left hand side, a great snake of smoke and mist, sweating monsters from between its scales.

"You understand, yes? You..."

I can barely breathe, barely speak through the drunken, heady swell of it all. He smiles through myriad mouths that lightly bite my chest and shoulder, that clamp leech-like to my neck.

"Yes," he tremors, turning my eyes up to his, forcing me to watch them blaze. "Yes, I understand."

I've rarely met another of my peculiar kind (Morrow being the grandest exception). I don't know their protocols when it comes to lovers, the children they pluck like fruit from the bough. But I will not take them by force or deceit. They have to *know*, to understand. Don't mistake me, it isn't some moral qualm on my part. Rather a preoccupation with cultivating the perfect experience, a communion the memory of which will sustain for days or months to come. It's better for us both if they come willingly, understand what's going to happen and celebrate in it.

We kiss through a haze of wine, tasting sweet and sour on one another's palates. He burns inside, as they all do, his corpse-pallor masking something more vital: the memories of old loves that ride on his spit mine to savour, as is the taste of blood from their abuses, games that have gone too far, dependencies that have revealed themselves in all their cruelty. I feel blows that were meant in play but that split his lip, others that come through a haze of fury and disgust, spittle raining down to mingle with the blood he drools and weeps, silent prayers that this will be the last disgrace before silence takes him.

And I let him have a sliver of me, a tendril unspooling, delivering sweet nectar onto his tongue. He shudders against me, almost convulsing, as he tastes a whisper of what I am, finds himself in the places of old loves who have gone before.

"Shit. *Shit.*"

I laugh, running fingers through his hair, raking the protuberant contours and angles of his back. He arches like a cat against the attention, inviting deeper cuts.

"Is it what you expected? Is it what you want?"

I don't need him to say it. I hear it, feel it, the song he sings communicating need more eloquently than any words: *Take me. Love me. Open me. Teach me to fly.*

But I want to hear him say it.

"Yes. *Yes.*"

I smile against his smile, biting his lip, drawing a little blood. The taste is intoxicating, the songs and stories it carries even more so.

No more waiting. No more want. My body bleeds, though he cannot see it. I am so open, so wounded, the air makes me tremble, the disturbance of his breath and heart-beat enough to almost excite orgasm.

Hoisting him up, I lay him down before the fire, the boy writhing in the gentle glow, eager to be naked, to be seen and consumed. I strip him slowly, ritualistically, tongues both seen and unseen following in my finger's wake, tasting so much more than the chemicals in his sweat. Not even a lover would know him like this, every forbidden fantasy, every momentary, idle imagining. Every twitch and tremor and strange habit. Mine, all mine. His song thrills, the boy piercing me with it, eruptions of pale silver, streamers of moonlight, licking my wounds, carrying his confessions, all that he is, was or might be. I bloat, barely able to hold onto my mask of humanity. It wavers before his eyes, shifting on the bone. I try to hold onto it, for his sake, but the song is too sweet, too sumptuous.

Some of them have screamed upon witnessing the truth of me. Some have kicked and raked out, attempting to flee. Sour notes in the honey. Others, the least satisfying by far, have simply surrendered, becoming meek and suicidal. He does neither.

Smiling, he stares, rearing up, singing all the more sweetly, giving me his elegies. This is his now, the final verse. He draws me into a kiss that carries his every suicide: those contemplated, those conducted, in other whens and wheres. He sees the monster, knows it and wants it, as he always has, ever since those first unwanted nights when he lay enveloped in black omens of the life that was to come, the sanity-shredding horror of being caged inside a skull that would never allow him to fly free, a skin that would always constrict and chafe and disappoint.

I almost can't contain him, almost can't take what he has to give. A feast to glut armies, congregations of starving faithful. All mine. *All mine.*

The song shreds reality around us, causing it to flicker and distort. Shadows swell, the walls draw away and old, alien moons shine their light down on us as I draw his legs up, entering him.

There is pain. There's always pain, for us both. But he's an old hand at this perversion, practised a thousand times over, a vessel for the sin that entire bloodlines have been put to the flames for in more ignorant centuries. Here, a communion, a rite beyond any proscribed sacrament. He burns inside, a molten thing, a furnace. I can barely keep myself together as the song resounds and swells and washes through me. The days unlived, the nights undreamed, all experienced here, in these sweating instants, these gasped and grunted breaths. He is murdered, stabbed and throttled by his lovers. He murders them in his turn, biting out their throats, smashing their skulls as they lie panting over him. Confessions of love come just as profusely, weeping and gasping, riding waves of orgasm that ripple out into the surrounding darkness.

I am all of them, and so is he. We lose ourselves and one another, all distinction dissolving. This is it, the exquisite apotheosis that I seek, the communion that dissolves us, returns us to that original, chemical condition, in which we swill together, becoming expressions of one another's potential.

He aches for it. Begs for it. A climax to eclipse all others, a sensation that will undo all he has ever presumed of pleasure.

And the beast will no longer be denied.

The mask of humanity gives way and he sees me at last. I bite, tearing into his throat with fangs long and sharp enough to puncture clean through, shearing arteries and windpipe and vertebrae, the hot eruption of his blood in my mouth, upon my face, an angel's rain; the same that invisibly baptised me in the night beyond. And still he gasps in his ecstasies, still he smiles, through blood and pain. This is how it was always meant to be, how the song ends in his every dream of it. I take him as I took the others before, make him part of that same choir.

We erupt as one, his semen hot against my underside, mine filling him to capacity. In that instant, we fly from this carnage, into a condition far purer; one that I know well from previous communions, from the angels I have made in blood and want. I carry him there, my teeth and talons in him, tasting not only blood, but the moonlight stuff of his soul. I know it's only temporary, that he'll be gone from me and the world very soon, into states and places I can only imagine, when one of my angels deigns to sing to me, when we make love in drug-fueled dreams.

He laughs as we soar, as stars and states of being stream by, as he leaves behind pain and disappointment and want. Everything that drove him into my arms, that I ache to taste, in this fleeting, ephemeral condition. I am pure here, too. A beast woven from the darkness between stars, the empty void, hungering, vacuous and eternal. I feel him inside of me, moonlight kindling in my belly, my mind, becoming raw potential: a meal of the days that will never be, the loves he will never know. Mine, now, saturating me, filling my emptiness. Some lovers fight to hold onto them, raking at me, struggling to free themselves. He does not. He embraces me, draws me deeper, inviting me to drink my fill.

And I do.

≈

WAKING IS a descent as awful as our shared flight was rapturous; he is gone from me without a word, without oaths of adoration, confessions of love. Wings erupt from his larval condition, more numerous and complex than those of any flesh-bound life, jeweled with burning eyes. In that instant, I have no choice but to let him go or be murdered by the fire in his gaze. He ascends, becoming invisible, intangible, one with the light, leaving nothing behind but the echoes of what he might have been had he lived, had the world proved worthy of him.

Ashes. The ashes of dead things. All my meals, my communions, my love affairs, come to this desolation in the end. He is no different.

Surrounded by echoes of our lover's song, I fall, my own wings tattered and insubstantial. Things of shadow that cannot bear me up, carry me into whatever plane of being awaits beyond unendurable eternity. I am so afraid, so terrified of what it might be. I can't allow myself to trespass there, not yet. Still so much a child myself, unable to grow, for fear of what adulthood might oblige.

The fall tears me, tatters me, my wings streaming away in black rivulets, until I tumble into the flesh that should have long, long since gone to mulch and dust, that has been murdered and undone more times than I recall and yet still moves and breathes, aches and lusts. Bloated, now. Filled to capacity like a tick, still buried in the ragged remains of the boy, in that cold and abattoir-stinking murk.

The fire has burned low, and he is still and cold beneath me. Weeping, drooling blood, I extricate myself from him, laying down his tattered carcass, forcing myself to witness the carnage I've wrought upon it.

No great loss. Not to me.

A distant whisper, a fleeting laugh. Maybe an angel's forgiveness, maybe nothing but the salving echo of my own guilt. Whatever the case, I ease myself free, still hard, still pulsing cold matter, that might have the capacity to make children for all I know, though of what deranged or diseased kind I shudder to imagine.

The house groans and creaks around me, the walls settling, faint ripples still passing through as though they're painted on curtains that stir in a cosmic breeze.

It is delicious. It is awful. His blood and meat swilling in my belly, a meal that will sustain for many, many moons to come. I need sleep, somewhere to dream and digest in peace. It can't be here. As atomised from one another as the neighbours are, some of the more curtain-twitching ilk will have seen us arrive, will take salacious delight in mentioning the youth of my companion to any willing to indulge their gossip. And the boy's friends will notice his absence, the shallow soul manning the bar where I found him, whose glares burned the back of my neck as I shepherded him out into the morning, others whose faces linger in his memory, that swirl and coalesce behind my eyes as our experiences intermingle, become one.

Old weariness stirs at the thought of what awaits. The end of one game, the beginning of another. Every communion an uprooting, a life abandoned. I won't lament this one in particular. It was a lonely, joyless thing. Even so, the play of stillness lasted longer than most, allowing me to grow used to certain comforts. I would take a moment to cleanse myself, allow the beast to recede, leave as discreetly as I may.

Not this time. It's been too long. I've forgotten the hideous, loathsome joy of it. The taste of blood on my tongue, the strength that pulses through my limbs, the raw *want* that still aches between my legs. There is potency in this, poetry beyond what any static and ephemeral life can imagine. I am a nightmare in the painted darkness, a million nameless senses blossoming, the world a garden of alien experience.

I SMELL the one in the dark, hear the frantic staccato of his heart. Petals of fire unfurl in the night, so short lived and yet, to my altered senses, slow and variegated as any blooming bird of paradise.

Pain. Rare and all-eclipsing, burning cold momentarily whiting out the world. I hear them singing together, my angels, as they make love somewhere beyond my reach or comprehension. Then, fragmented prayers muttered in broken, archaic Israeli, peppered with mispronounced Arabic. I recognise the abjurations, for all their ineloquence. Old, old verses, designed to wound my kind, to bind and render us impotent.

Through tears, through the living lights that dance across my swollen eyes, I see him, trembling as he advances. Ha! The taxi driver. I should've known. What is he? Some degenerate descendent of the old hunters, the Circles and their genocidal creeds? If so, a poor reflection of what their bloodlines have become. So afraid, I smell his sweat, the urine soaking his trousers, raw terror staining the air around him pellucid yellow.

Too quick with the prayers, too slow with the gun. He fires again, only this time, his shot is wildly off mark. Even were it not, it wouldn't have found me. The bullet already lodged in my shoulder erupts with spines of frost, anesthetic venom searing its way through my systems. A familiar disgrace, almost nostalgic in its rarity. I tear the wound open in the blink of an eye, ripping out the nub of flowering silver that shudders and smokes as I drop it to the ground. His prayers become more frantic the closer I approach, his eyes so wide as to start out of their sockets. He fires wildly, until the gun is empty. Lights flicker on in surrounding houses, voices call distantly from open windows. I'm on him in an instant, bearing him to the ground. Poor man. He hardly knew anything of this before tonight, had almost begun to believe that his Mother's stories were exactly that. The delusions of a mind slowly losing itself to hereditary dementia.

Now, he stares up into the face of childhood nightmares, everything he has been conditioned to define as evil since he spoke his first word, took his first step. His prayers and icons, things he has no true faith in, mean nothing. Inert on his tongue, cold in his hands. So, I take them both, his hands coming in a series of quick-silver bites, his tongue in a smothering kiss. I swallow it like a bloody oyster, prayers still trembling in the meat, though the throat that shaped them now fills with martyr's blood. Through it all, the filth of hatred and intended violence, I still taste him; the boy who so happily made a meal of himself, who has become something beyond this one's futile imagination.

"He, at least, has some joy now. For you, my love...Oh, for you, it will be terrible. That I promise."

I revel in the sound of my own voice, the joyous growls, the resonance in my belly, as though I've swallowed a roaring furnace or have become a hive of living and furious swarms. He will not die. Not yet, anyway. I know how to preserve them in their states of disgrace, their mindless despairs. Morrow taught me the trick of it, though I've never felt moved to practice it before. In this instance it will be a pleasure.

Taking him in my arms, I carry him into the failing night, where he and I will become rumour together. His laments will echo through the heads of the sleeping and unborn alike, making both equally reluctant to wake.

THE CITY BEHIND THE CITY

LC VON HESSEN

*A*t the western edge of Manhattan on a night like any other, Theodore stalked alone.

A recent rain had shellacked the streets and sidewalks with a dull wet gleam and the dank miasma of concrete-dirtied water still hung in the air. The encrusted grime of countless rubber soles and wheels and leaking garbage sacks had rinsed into the gutter, pooling at sewer grates clogged by the filth. Overhead, light pollution hid the stars under a sickly scrim of bruised violet-grey, the full moon curdling through like the contents of an acne pustule.

His wanderings led him where the tidy grid of Chelsea met the patchwork zigzag of Greenwich Village, pavement under his heels shifting abruptly to cobblestone: a Franken-steined mélange of weathered bricks and mirrored glass, a different, confused city growing a new crop of flesh after its many old skins had been burnt away, scraped off, surgically excised. Gutted caverns of former factories transformed into high-end boutiques with blank-faced mannequins posing at strict angles inside. Whitewashed yuppie galleries like—*no, not* that *one, don't think about it, don't even think its name*—in century-old warehouses that once held bootleggers' crates and butchers' carcasses.

Theodore turned up his trench coat collar and kept walking. A human shadow, a drifting flaneur, a generic young male NPC programmed to wander at random among detailed polygons, no backstory given: He could be anyone. He almost wished he'd taken up smoking so he could pause and drag a cigarette under a streetlight, capturing the existential swagger of Alain Delon or Pierre Clémenti and the coldly devastating sex appeal to go with it. He knew he'd be flattering himself to think he was *that* good-looking, though his features were pointed and regular enough to be considered handsome, if one was into ectomorphic, vaguely nerdy white boys.

He had gone to see a film in the Village earlier that evening and now had no particular destination in mind. Long walks alone always cleared his head, folding him into a set of senses, observing in silence. And they made him feel deliciously sinister: as though the hand in his trenchcoat pocket clutched a blood-caked stiletto instead of a crumpled Bible tract plucked from a subway bench.

Empty pockets of the old city, waiting. Theodore loved to catch sight of the many small, defunct details of old architectural façades: decorative symbols with esoteric meanings long forgotten, a hidden code etched in red clay and wrought iron. Echoes of years, decades, centuries of strife and jubilance, ghostly clues of unknown lives. The city was a haunted house writ large. He thought of the Regency-era graffiti carved into the Temple of Dendur at the Met, the initials' careful serifs. Long after bones crumbled, headstones wore away: *I was here, I existed.*

Theodore had gone to a college full of pseudo-Brutalist architecture and, in retrospect, he truly believed it had exacerbated his chronic depression: four years living among featureless brown brick slabs looming everywhichwhere, trudging to class against this backdrop that resembled a penal colony from some dreary dystopian film he'd watch between bong hits. In his final year, a new hyper-modern building of tinted glass and painted metal had been erected in the hope of adding some color and character to the campus, though it only succeeded in resembling a jaunty cocktail umbrella jabbed into a mound of dog shit.

He lamented New York City's ongoing, arduous transformation into a city clean and dull, appealing to the studied minimalism of the absurdly rich.

Still nestled in Theodore's unconscious was the platonic ideal of The City: not just "the city," that tri-county slang for Manhattan, but The City Behind The City. What it might have been, what it could have become. The Manhattan of his longtime dreams and daydreams. The rollercoaster of a monorail looping around a sprawl of gleaming iridescent Boschian spires and enormous half-sunken silver statues at the juncture of East and Hudson Rivers. The massive windows onto equally-massive brass gears rotating human-sized clockwork jesters and devils for the wonder of passersby. The step pyramid in the midst of Midtown topped with an ivy-clotted plateau of colonial tombs where impossibly tall, lean living Deco sculptures bent low to whisper in his ear.

These visions coexisted with a City informed by seedy accounts outmoded decades ago, junkies and whores and No Wave squats, leather, needles, knives, neon. Several years ago Theodore, fresh from his first commute through Grand Central, had snickered at the sign for Pershing Square since he knew of it as a former male hustler haunt described in *City of Night*, not recalling until years later that *that* Pershing Square was on the other coast. Nonetheless, this fictional history formed yet another wax exhibit in his mental museum.

To teenage Theodore half a country away, The City, with

its perpetual lights visible from afar in the depths of night and the heights of the air, had been a cluster of jewels on black velvet, a galaxy pinned down; a symbol of independence, creative success, and willing debauchery. The City in its dream-state had been a promise out of the suburbs, away from the shithead jocks who wielded *faggot* like a melee weapon. He'd wanted to punch them, kick them in the balls, every time it crossed his ears, directed at him or otherwise. He'd wanted not to be angry all the time, not any more.

The streets in this part of town were largely and thankfully empty. He passed a pair of twenty-something tourist women with hair and skin dyed roughly the same shade of wheat-beige, drunk on a weekend evening, sharing an uneven gait. One of them, with the glossy, unfocused eyes and slackened lips of a beached fish, loosely clutched a pink rhinestone-encrusted phone, which threatened to clatter from her hand into a murky puddle beside her kitten heels.

"If we can't find a Starbucks open," her companion insisted, "you can just go on the train. There's *always* a toilet on the train."

Theodore smiled to himself, said nothing, walked on. He recalled the late-night ride home in which he'd heard a tell-tale sploshing sound at the back of the subway car, had turned his head to see a tall man standing in the corner, facing the walls, with a transparent pool spreading around his sneakers. He'd caught the eye of a young bearded man also bearing witness, who'd silently shaken his head at Theodore and smiled. What, after all, could they *do?*

A pair of dingy sleeping bags hugged a shuttered storefront like pupae, one lump shifting under a handwritten sign on torn cardboard. The city's homeless were, yet again, transformed into set pieces, even more invisible than Theodore himself. He, too, was currently unemployed, had been for months now. There but for the grace...

And there, the westernmost edge of the city, a view of the

choppy obsidian skin of the river. He had given serious consideration one night to climbing over the railing and giving himself to the sea after all that transpired, after those two successive blows—

But that's not how I want to die.

He turned his back on the water. In a narrow, wedge-shaped vacant lot between a hotel skyscraper and a yuppie-priced bistro, Theodore saw an astronaut. No: a Victorian deep-sea diver. He stepped closer to the chain-link fence and peered through the dark. Alongside the prop diving suit was a human-sized bronze Statue of Liberty hoisting an American flag which draped over the face of a knight gripping a Claymore, both flanked by a car from the Depression era. A requisite no trespassing sign was posted on the metal links overhead. Theodore smiled: a vestige of old, weird New York. Some elderly eccentric living nearby must rent out props for plays and film shoots.

—Ramon meeting up with him at their usual bar after work, sharing photos of himself as a zombie, as a cop, as a stubble-chinned leather-jacketed tough bastard hilariously referred to in the casting notice as a "rocker;" whatever that day's shoot demanded—

Great. Now he'd done it.

—Ramon jokingly attempting to teach him the wrong meanings of words in Spanish, occasionally foiled by the New York Spanglish Theodore had picked up by osmosis after years living in Brooklyn, like when he tried to claim pendejo *meant* handsome—

—Ramon surprising him with a birthday present from the Morbid Anatomy gift shop: a taxidermied little white mouse in a cubicle, facing a laptop with a miniature cup of coffee beside its paw. "That's you, you know." His naughty, naughty grin—

—Ramon's hand snaking around his waist at the edge of the pit during a metal show at St. Vitus—

And he realized. This was the hotel.

The hotel.

The sort of hotel where middle-aged bridge-and-tunnel businessmen had encounters with their bored mistresses and used their expense accounts to buy sex work. Its aesthetic was an early-aughts rendition of a 1970s rendition of The Future. He and Ramon had booked a room for a night, celebrating Ramon's official qualification for SAG membership. They'd pretended to be decadent businessmen on a corporate retreat, Messrs. Buchner and Escolar, Esqs. Ramon in his teal suit and Tom Ford cologne, unwrapping each other before an entire wall made of window-glass overlooking the highway and the Hudson, the Jersey skyline. Tenderness and violence on blanched white sheets, then sharing a bathtub behind a transparent glass wall, then dirtying the sheets even further. That wicked gleam in Ramon's dark eyes: *Why don't we come back here sometime and bring a third?* Oh yes, a delicious and frankly obvious idea. But in retrospect—

Were you thinking of him *even then?*

A well-trod anger flared up in Theodore's mind and immediately drained him weary.

This walk was a mistake. Too many ghosts.

He turned around to head back to the subway, go home. Largely unfamiliar with this part of the city, he soon lost his bearings as the streets split and cracked into each other, painful stretches of cobbled and pitch-coated skin. Along the way, he passed yet another gutted warehouse. He assumed it was a hotel lobby at first, all brass and glass and weathered brick. But the further he walked, the more he realized it was a set of open-plan roomlets, all in a row, and all minor variations on the same assemblage.

Two couches, almost-black and off-white, parallel to a central coffee table topped with a potted succulent or oversized hardcover book with a blank cover. A hanging lamp or modernist chandelier overhead. An end table or faux fireplace on the flanking wall, bracketed by a pair of long mirrors, each in turn fronted by a copy of an ancient sculpture: Chinese lion-dogs, Greco-Roman sphinxes, Hercules encircled by a serpent.

—*Ramon sliding his hands into Theodore's back pockets, both at once, his strong arms—*

No!

"Theodore Buchner!" A man's voice called behind him. "Are you still interested in the position?"

Theodore turned around, utterly baffled.

The position?

True, he had sent out a number of job applications in the past several months, to the extent that he had no idea which position was being referenced. And the man did know his name, first and last. His picture was available online, a calm headshot affixed to his public CV, all quite professional. It was entirely possible, if unusual, that he'd been recognized.

The man offering *the position* stood before the great glass doors of the not-hotel in a nondescript brown suit and tie— the color, Theodore thought uncharitably, of a robust morning shit. A lanky man, with a nose that looked broken from an incident he'd never speak of, and low-set hairy brows like a pair of mice nestled in his sockets.

"Name's Jon Lund–that's J-O-N, no H, no extraneous letters! Lund, L-U-N-D, just the way it sounds!" He grinned and held out a hand, pressed Theodore's own with unnecessary firmness. "Care to have a step inside and chat about the position? Serendipitous timing, don't'cha think?"

"Uh, yeah. Sure."

Theodore wasn't sure about any of this, but it was starting to drizzle. His phone was dead and he was still unsure of the exact route back to the subway. And if this *was* a real opportunity, he might as well. His savings were drained to the dregs. He badly needed the money.

Following Jon Lund through the doorway brought Theodore into an Ikea take on Art Deco with classical accents, bedecked in the gloss and flash of modernity. A central chandelier of dangling glass shards and a string of its diminutive copies casting pools of light and dramatic shadows across a polished marble floor in shades of old bone. A ceiling high enough to reveal a vastness of space, but still low and dark enough to conceal its true breadth. And all around him, a huge spread of little lounges in a seemingly infinite grid. What *was* this? An oddly grand reception area? Certainly not the office itself?

"Come, come, Theodore!" Mr. Lund gestured him forward. "It *is* Theodore—Ted? Teddy?"

"Just Theodore."

He was definitely a Theodore. Not a Ted or a Teddy or, despite a short-lived attempt in his sophomore year of high school, a Theo.

This was inordinately pleasing to Jon Lund. "*Thee*-o-dore! All three syllables!" His palms met in a trio of golf claps. "Well done! I approve!"

"Uh, thanks."

"And it is, I expect, *Byook*-ner, like a stern rebuke, not *Buck*-ner, like 'buckle your seatbelt, kiddo!'?"

"Yep. That's right."

"Right! Right! Right this way! Come along now!" Mr. Lund brushed past the bust of a curly-haired noseless man. "Now, it's a short-term opportunity for an independent contractor, mind you," said the man as he walked, "but pending our needs—and your performance, of course—it could very well turn into something permanent. Would that suit you, Theodore?"

"Yeah, definitely." He realized the man hadn't mentioned the name of his company. Theodore, of course, had no time or opportunity to research and hoped he wouldn't make an utter ass of himself.

He silently prepared his tongue to emit some horrid tech-nobabble about *experiential brand influence leveraging syner-*

gistic paradigm disruption for topline born-mobile presence solutions as ideate bandwidth to innovative tech rockstar wizardry.

Theodore discreetly assessed himself in the many passing mirrors as Lund led him in zigzag fashion through the empty roomlets. He was wearing a short-sleeved dress shirt under his trenchcoat, a decent pair of trousers, and generic black shoes that were only lightly scuffed. He patted his dark hair: no strands must be frizzled or unkempt. In his roiling anxiety, the statues all appeared to be facing him, appraising with their cold stone eyes.

As he walked, Jon Lund kept up a running stream of generic work patter for which Theodore was only required to give an occasional monosyllabic response. Theodore briefly caught sight of the first other human he'd seen in this building: an older man on a couch, nodding his head at Theodore and lifting his glass of whiskey in silent cheers.

He realized then how far he must be from the windows, the entrance, of which he could see nothing.

Mr. Lund kept on talking.

"Ever heard of the Old Tannery? It was only a few blocks from here, built in the colonial era. Then when the tannery closed down, the underground level was turned into a tenement. Used to call it the Devil's Den: the worst den of debauchery this city has ever seen! No furniture, no windows, everyone fumbling about in the dark. No plumbing in those days! The stink of piss everywhere! Children were born and died in there, children who lived their whole short lives never seeing sunlight. Constant sex and rape and murder! All those bodies, living and dead, fused into one big, naked mass after awhile, I expect. Biggest scandal since the Doctors' Riot of 1788. And some years later it was bought up by a reverend and turned into a Christian mission. They just paved over the tenement doors, with all those bodies still inside, alive and otherwise. Who knows what's still down there, eh? *Eh?* You know, you *know*, Theodore, the City has a long memory. Ah! Here we are."

Lund spread out his arm before a roomlet that appeared no different than any other.

Theodore sat on the nearest couch and removed his trench coat as the man absented himself behind a wall. Theodore drummed his fingers atop his knee. Perhaps now Mr. Lund was going to wheel out the whiteboard and ask him to write needlessly convoluted lines of code in order to prove his worth. Or perhaps he'd have to write it in lipstick on one of the mirrors adjacent. Was this what they called a *non-traditional workplace?*

Across from him, a pair of nude, broken male torsos stared down impassively from granite slabs. Showroom dummies.

Everything glistened but the statues. Even the dull gleam of the Naugahyde couch, upon which his shifting ass and thighs squelched out sounds uncomfortably close to flatulence. The glass coffee table was a particular fingerprint trap. This would make a good coke table, he thought.

—*Dividing up bitter-tasting pills of MDMA with Ramon Escolar*—

Fucking hell.

They spoke of "lots of fish in the sea" when trying to cheer up the newly-single, as if the mysterious X factor of Romance was an immutable code to be deciphered, as if the right combination of shared glances and properly timed laughs and whatnot could make *anyone* fall in love with *anyone* if one was only patient, or else unleash a sudden, gripping mutual love like a cracked can of mustard gas tossed into a trench. Because they both shared basic physical attraction and facile interests like sports teams or favorite sitcoms and were both Nice People who were Nice to each other and didn't have Issues. This, to most people, was love.

Ramon had loved his strangeness, didn't merely tolerate it

for the sake of his Nice parts. Theodore had been beyond lucky to find this once, and before he was 30 no less. He would not find it again.

If Ramon had even truly loved him, after it all, *considering*. Theodore didn't know which was the worse prospect: that he had been loved imperfectly—no, *deceptively*—or that he had merely deluded himself into believing he'd known love in the first place.

But this was a bad track to go down, especially now. He'd had nothing to eat for dinner but overpriced movie theatre popcorn and a bottle of soda he'd snuck in through a trench coat pocket to save money. He was starting to feel light-headed. He feared the onset of what he deemed a malnourishment migraine, a familiar condition when doing long hours of overtime at his work computer fueled only by steady cups of generic break-room coffee.

When you don't eat a balanced diet, your psych meds don't work properly.

A low prickling in his ears: the susurration of whispers. He stood, looking around for the source. It was loudest at the facing wall. *The statues.* He craned his ear towards one quadriplegic torso. Yes, he couldn't make out any words, but there must be a hidden speaker inside—

"Your last job, Theodore!" Mr. Lund startled. "What was it, and why did you leave?"

Grasping his composure, Theodore said, "Oh! Uhhh. I worked for a video game company. Ochre Hill Games in Williamsburg. I was a texture artist, backgrounds mostly."

A hank of hair, about three strands at least an inch long, jutted from a skin tag in Lund's neck. It bothered Theodore immensely. He wished for a pair of tweezers.

"The biggest project that I worked on was *Hastur's Meridian*, which was an open-world RPG. It got good reviews and made it on some best-of lists that year, so I was pretty proud of that. But it didn't—sales weren't up to the projected level. And then the most recent game I worked on was *H: Devil's Echo*, which, uh, didn't do so well."

And then there were those lawsuits. Best not bring that up. Nothing to do with me, anyway.

"So because of those profit losses, the company shut down, and we all got laid off."

With only two weeks of severance pay, and after signing a legal contract promising not to shit-talk the company in public. Fuckers.

"I, uh. I have an online portfolio, if you—"

"Ogre Hill!" said Mr. Lund. Or perhaps he said it correctly and Theodore had merely misheard, and would thus look like a pedantic asshole for daring to correcting him. "Now, what *didn't* you like about Ogre Hill? What was your least favorite part of the job? What *really* pissed you off?"

Christ, where to start? The long hours of crunch time and the impossibility of making evening plans with any sort of encroaching project deadline? The absurd secrecy surrounding the company's products, even beyond a typical NDA? The utter lack of job security, especially because NYC was clotted with creative degrees, fresh out of college and too young and green to know their worth? He couldn't be honest. Nobody was honest if they wanted to make a living, especially not in this city.

He opened his mouth to answer.

"One moment! Wait one moment, Theodore Buchner!" Jon Lund strode off again, with an elbow bent and an index finger in the air like a cartoon waiter. "A message for Mr. Cadmon! A *very important* missive! Now where did he—"

Lund's footsteps disappeared. Confused, Theodore meandered around the space, looking around. In a diagonally-adjacent roomlet, he saw the back of a standing man who was, yes, clearly pissing into a vase held up to his crotch, the sound of a forceful stream echoing hollow inside the metal. The man's arm waggled twice, presumably shaking off the last drops. He zipped up his fly and replaced the urine-filled vase on the nearest end table. Noticing Theodore, he held a finger to his lips with a conspiratorial, if sheepish, smile.

"Little trick I learned." A rough, ill-exercised voice, followed by a series of dry coughs.

"So you don't know where the restroom is?"

The man shrugged. "Hell if I know. And good luck finding your way back."

He stood at the edge of the roomlet, shook his head, mimed a knock on an invisible wall. A sadness in his smile. Theodore recognized him now as the same man who'd raised a glass in his direction earlier. And furthermore, he recognized the man from *somewhere else*, somewhere unknown, an itch in the brain. Perhaps an ignored message on a dating app from a user who had, in turn, ignored his age limit?

The guy was at least twice Theodore's age, fifty-something, maybe even early sixties, but decently well-preserved. He was dressed in business casual, not much different from Theodore's own attire, though his right sleeve was torn above a crescent-shaped scar on his upper arm. He had the beginnings of a paunch straining his belt, was otherwise relatively slim. Dark hair, dusted with grey, parted sharply in a vain attempt to conceal the retreat of his hairline. Deep crows' feet stamping the corners of his eyes, ventriloquist lines loping from his nostrils to upper lip. No smile lines. The pallor of a career spent under fluorescent lights.

His eyes flicked about nervously. "Ah, well. He'll be back any time. I should leave you to it." He waved weakly and sat down, his back to Theodore, who returned to his own couch.

Despite his passivity, there was something strangely magnetic about that man, thought Theodore. Always wondered what it might be like, a man that much older, brazenly playing with him like a ripe young doll...

For fuck's sake, Theodore, you're at an interview. He told himself this, but it was on the verge of laughter. *You've worked with fucking weirdos before. Like* you're *not a fucking weirdo.* How he'd glance into strangers' windows on the sly during his walks, mentally photographing their décor, playing the role of a prospective home intruder. How he'd wonder what it would be like to slash a stranger's throat as he passed them on the sidewalk, just one quick slice, not changing his pace, not looking back.

He couldn't—*literally* couldn't—afford to be too picky. It had been hard enough to find his last job. Did he want to make minimum fucking wage again? Part-time job, no insurance? Routinely scolded by purse-lipped old bitches for being insufficiently obsequious? Falsely pointed out by parents of young children as a warning, the product of not going to college or getting good grades? Talked down to by managers who assumed he'd be nothing but a dumb-as-bricks workhorse?

Once again, here was Failure prodding its cold pistol barrel into his neck. Multivalenced failure. Failure in love and war, if the job market could be described as war (and in this city it certainly could).

Around the same time he lost his job at Ochre Hill, Ramon had left him for his ex, Jaecen. Well, essentially. They'd been messing about behind Theodore's back—perhaps they always had, perhaps it never ended when their relationship did—and he'd blown up and dumped Ramon once he found hard proof. Clearly Theodore was the aggrieved party here.

He had never liked the man. First time they'd met, Theodore at Ramon's side, Jaecen had given him an up-and-down once-over and ignored him from then on, summarily dismissing him without a word, a little lord reflexively shunning an inferior roll of damask in the bustling arms of a housemaid. But Ramon had been with Jaecen for seven years; Theodore was foolish to think he could ever compete with that.

Jaecen and Ramon were co-owners of a little avant-garde storefront gallery, a relic of their old relationship, mainly a venue to display Jaecen's art. Jaecen was among the broken baby dolls, neon face paint, and meme-worthy slogans strain of *artiste*. Jaecen with his overly sharp nostrils and prominent septum ring dangling like a bull's, his elongated horse face and stupid hip haircut halfway between a Danny Torrance bowl cut and a monk's tonsure, his trendy amorphous smocks making his body resemble a Mari Lwyd. Fuck, it's not even like he was *sexier* than Theodore.

And Ramon would pout and roll his eyes when Theodore questioned their *friendship*, that defensive stance so many men had about their long-term exes, whether tending an old flame or still fucking on the sly. *Like, I bet you were, Ramon, you were just* business partners. *Sure, it was a just-friends blowjob! Sharing dicks, like friends do! Just needed some cum stains on the floor for Jaecen's latest installation!*

Theodore hadn't had a serious boyfriend before, though he knew a lot of guys were friends with their exes, especially if their exes were also men, since it was a small fucking world even in a city of millions; and thus, for a long time, Theodore didn't know quite what was truly suspect and whether his own neuroticism was casting aspersions on something totally innocent. And that was his own undoing.

We were talking about moving in together, *for fuck's sake. I've never, I will never—*

A pale, sloppy woman teetered in heels towards Theodore's couch. Her birdlike features were framed by a blonde Marilyn Monroe hairdo, possibly a wig as it hung slightly askew. Her snug red cocktail dress matched the lipstick smeared up under her left cheekbone like a half-finished Glasgow smile. She bumped into the coffee table, hoisting the martini glass in her hand to save its contents, before collapsing on the couch beside Theodore and thrusting the drink in his face.

"Have a tipple for Mimsy," she slurred.

"Now now, we'll have enough of that, Miriam. It's not that time yet." Mr. Lund strode back in, clearly pissed off.

She blinked hard, trying to focus. "Johnny? 'S 'at you?"

"Jon *Lund*. Like *lunge*." He plucked the glass from her hand. A dollop of liquid sloshed onto the carpet below the table. From the stain arose, curiously, a thin trail of smoke.

"This isn't your narrative, Mim." A hollowness knocked on the tiles as he hauled her to her feet. Her dress ruched up at the thighs and Theodore saw that, beneath her pantyhose, she had an artificial leg. "Go with the piano man."

Theodore noticed, for the first time, the ambient piano loop echoing in the background. And the sound of a steady stream: not from a clandestine piss this time, but an indoor fountain. Potted ferns and palms accentuated the space, placed by unseen hands. The building was waking up.

"Now, Theodore." Lund sat down, uncomfortably close to him. He had no room to scoot away. "Theodore *Byook*-ner, like *Buch*enwald, not *Buck*-ner, like 'the buck stops here!'"

Whoa, what the fuck?

"So, you left Ichor Hill." Lund steepled his fingers over one crossed knee. "And then what? What else've you done for money since then?"

He immediately thought of the paid psych experiment at that clinic on the Upper East Side. He'd relinquished his coins and jewelry to lie in an MRI scanner while a series of disturbing photographs were flashed onscreen above him. If they caused him distress, the testers instructed, he was to tell himself that the contents of the image happened long ago or far away. He'd wonder, later, where these photos came from. A wild-eyed convict in court with his mouth duct-taped shut. A malnourished Russian child smoking meth. A young man kissing a dead body of indeterminate sex.

"I . . . just some freelance work."

"And what does your father do for a living?"

"Well, actually—uh, he died of heart disease a few years back."

"Ah, a widow's son!"

"Sure." Lund was quickly shifting from peculiar to offensive.

He paused, eyes grown thoughtful. "*Esss*-co-lar. Not a very *American* name, is it?"

"Excuse me?"

"Everyone is so sensitive nowadays." Lund laughed. And firmly, deliberately, squeezed his upper thigh.

The scene froze. Theodore felt the churning of blood in his body, the cold epiphany that everything here was Wrong.

What even was the position?

"I have to go to the restroom," he muttered, pushing himself off the couch, rushing through the roomlets.

Behind him, Jon Lund cackled.

Weaving past empty couches and statue plinths, Theodore ran right into a young man wearing leather goggles with the eyes blacked over like horse blinders. Theodore's first thought was of VR goggles, and how one couldn't wear them for long periods without nausea. The man wore wavy auburn hair and suspenders with an old-timey stiff collar. He smiled with too much gum, was passably handsome otherwise.

"Oh, pleased to meet you, Mr. Buchner." His pale, spidery fingers traced Theodore's face, his neck, his upper chest. It was strangely erotic.

"A message from Mr. Cadmon. Ah, that's me." His hands kept roaming. "It's only part of your initiation. It's only a test. Just a formality. You've already made it." A hand patted Theodore's groin and lingered slightly, feeling his embarrassing stirrings of arousal.

"Hmm. Look out for the Other Theodore. Look out, old man." Cadmon patted his shoulder, half in reassurance, half propelling him on his way.

The whispering of the statues had converged into a high-pitched *eeee*.

He leaned near an Apollo to listen and caught himself in the mirror. He wasn't smiling.

But his reflection certainly was.

Smiling so wide, in fact, that his lips—bared on sharp, grey, triangular teeth—split open at the corners and peeled back to the cheekbones.

Theodore turned to run, but not fast enough. A piercing pain lit into his right arm just below the shoulder, tearing his sleeve in two and a howl from his lungs. He pressed his palm to the wound, attempting to staunch the blood from the jagged crescent in his flesh.

Lund's cackle again. He ran.

Theodore ran through the grid, across the grand chessboard. Other people appeared at times, but were quite unable to help him. They were otherwise occupied enacting their own hells through the mirrors.

Here, a man like a slab with a pelican's jowl crushed skulls of desiccated, doll-sized bodies in his massive fist. From each skull, white-gold beetles swarmed over his tuxedo and into his waiting mouth. The woman in red—Mimsy? Miriam?—stumbled out, sobbing.

A sharp gun-pop and this mirror was abruptly coated with blood, though completely dry on Theodore's side. A person-shaped puppet sank down through the gore.

Here, a man covered in grime from his prominent sideburns to his balloon sleeves removed wet human skins from a wooden barrel and clothes-pinned them to a drooping line.

And everywhere, statues pulsing, squirming, cracking their stone, flesh rippling through, aching to be born or else properly die.

Theodore collapsed on a random couch, exhausted and lost. His arm throbbed under a sticky veil of dried blood.

A loud, wet crunch and he turned to see the dark-haired

older man seated in the next roomlet over. His whiskey glass had been swapped out for a chalice, inside which was the coiled body of a small green serpent whose head the man had just bitten off.

"'S an acquired taste," he said, swallowing. "Hey, don't worry about Lund. He's not the boss. He doesn't run anything. He doesn't even run his nose. He's just here."

"What about you?"

"I'm just here, too." He swept his arm in a broad hemisphere. "We're all...*here*." He flicked his eyes down at Theodore's crotch, then back to his face. Subtle, but unmistakable. "A little pent-up?"

"Excuse me?"

"Cadmon's usually up for it, if you can catch him. Or, if you want..." He smirked and cocked his head.

Despite all this madness, Theodore was tempted. It had been a few months. Not since a too-quick restroom fuck with a wedding photographer he'd wanted to see again, who never messaged back.

But before he could step forward, the Theodore in the mirror did first.

He watched himself, there in the mirror, sitting in the man's lap, on his thigh, kissing, neck bitten, their shirts unbuttoned, flies undone, hands winking inside, cocks out, the man lolling his tongue around Theodore's erection, two fingers up his ass, Theodore straddling his lap and pinioning his hips, guiding him inside, their torn sleeves riding up, matching crescent scars, one raw, one shiny and smooth. He was profoundly aroused by the sight. He reached for his zipper. He bit his lip and his sharp teeth drew blood.

"Never get caught in your own reflection, Theodore."

Lund stepped forward, hands clasped.

"Oh yes, we know all about you. Tracking your dirt into our clean establishment." He pointed at Theodore's shoes, which were in fact dry. "You showed insufficient gratitude.

145

You must say thank you after every question. Many would die for the position, you know. Many would kill for it. Say thank you. Say *thank you.*" Lund gritted his teeth.

"But you've already been accepted. Yes. And you'll never get anywhere else like that. You'll never...go anywhere...*else.*"

Behind Lund in the mirror, the Other Theodore spread his arms, and the severed heads of Ramon and Jaecen plopped down at his feet.

But Theodore wasn't afraid or disgusted. He liked it. *Liked it.*

After he lost his job and his man he'd fantasize, constantly, obsessively, of going on set or to the gallery, a faceless cipher with a concealed weapon. A gunshot to that pretty face. A knife through that shapeless smock. They would think it was performance art. Karo syrup from a squib. Brilliant effects, really. Drifting out the door before—

Heheheee! Heeeehehee! The Other Theodore had shrunken their heads down and planted them on sticks, one in each fist. The Other Theodore made Jaecen's head whinny and neigh, made Ramon's head blather in stentorian Thespianese. The gore from their necks made red mittens of his hands.

He liked it.

And a cold sweat gripped Theodore:

He was right to leave me.

I'm an awful, awful man.

Not for any of his words, thoughts, or deeds, necessarily, but an innate awfulness, a repulsion, specific to Theodore Buchner alone. The voice from the oubliette was right, had been all along.

The older man, alone now, smiled at him, beaming, blissful in a more-than-post-coital sense.

"Perhaps," he said, "I can leave now."

He donned his trench coat and stood on the table, where his belt had been slung on a loop from the chandelier above.

He nestled the loop around his neck and winked at Theodore. And jumped.

You'll be forgotten to history, you know.

(Was the voice his? The Other Theodore? The older Theodore?)

But you're a part of The City now. And The City won't forget you.

He sat down to wait.

He would wait for a long time.

But at least The City had a long memory.

THERIANTHROPE

BRIAR RIPLEY PAGE

*E*ven a man who's pure at heart and says his prayers by night, they say. And you aren't a man. And you were raised an atheist. And you've never been pure of heart. Your heart is a dark, hateful engine. It fuels your four padded feet as they tear down the sidewalk after the screaming woman. Tiffany. Sandy hair, fashionably layered. Suit jacket. Gold jewelry. It's not yet 6 p.m., but you can see the moon in the daylight sky. Passersby gawk at you and scramble for cover and hold up their phones to take videos, but no one tries to help Tiffany.

Her ankles wobble. It must be hard to run in those heels. You tense your hindquarters and spring as she tumbles to the concrete floor of the world. You can smell her fear, cold and sour, spiced by a faint, piquant note of subconscious arousal.

You've never felt so much like yourself.

WHEN YOU WERE A BABY, you never stopped crying. You couldn't sleep. You were born with a canine tooth already grown in and a head already thatched with black hair. As you grew, you remained a fretful insomniac. Your other teeth came in early and they came in sharp. Your father, who was a dentist, was proud. Your mother, who was not a dentist, was worried. She gave you a baby doll to play with, an expensive one the size of a real baby, with soft skin and a pursed mouth with a hole that you were supposed to pour water into. The doll even had a diaper to change.

"I always wanted something like this when I was a little girl," your mother said, smiling at you expectantly. You held the doll by one leg, making her open-and-shut eyelids flutter. She had a pleasant texture, squishy yet firm. Your mouth itched as you smiled back, but you knew enough to wait for your mother to leave to bite down on the doll's leg. Chewing her to a pulp was heaven. You worked your way slowly up her body for two weeks, then shoved her spit-soaked remains in a box under your bed. You told your mother she was lost. Your mother seemed to buy it, but she never gave you a doll again.

A little later, when you were not quite five, you had an accident. At a neighborhood barbecue, you tried to play with a stranger's nervous husky. You growled at him, grabbed his ears ungently. That was the kind of goblin child you were.

You don't remember the moment he attacked, but you remember the shock of blood, the smell of spit and animal fear up close, your breath and the dog's breath entwined as though you had always been connected by teeth and pain and terror, and always would be. You remember a wet, loud sensation that filled you up and drowned all your usual thoughts and feelings. You couldn't tell if you were screaming or not, but you must have been, because you heard running feet and adult voices and then you heard thuds and scared yelps and the dog wasn't on you anymore. You felt the absence of his weight as almost a loss, and your vision was a haze of red.

Then you were in the hospital, and your head felt huge

and numb, and you couldn't see out of your right eye. Your mother was holding your hand. She wouldn't look at you, but she gripped your fingers so hard they started to go as numb as your face.

Miraculously, there was very little permanent scarring. You were under the impression for many years that the dog had eaten your eye, but you found out as a teenager it had to be surgically removed when you were in the hospital. Punctured and lacerated, infected, rotting inside your head. You have no memory of this. A mental image that has persisted in your daydreams and nightmares for twenty years is of dog teeth fitting themselves around the jelly of your eyeball. You imagine the dog's furred throat moving as it swallows your sight, taking your perspective into itself.

You never hated dogs. You understood the husky. An eyeball would be more satisfying to bite than any doll's plastic flesh.

It was difficult adjusting to the loss of your stereoscopic vision, but by midway through elementary school you couldn't remember what it was like to have it. You didn't mind your glass eye. You minded the way other kids gawked at you and teased you and ostracized you. Maybe that wasn't really because of the eye. Maybe the eye was just a convenient excuse.

Maybe it was because they sensed something wicked growing inside you. You sensed it, too. It lay in the cage of your ribs like a bristling animal. It sent thick black filaments running through your muscles, making them twitch. You felt the filaments brushing against the back of your skin at night and you knew that one day soon they'd erupt into fur. You dreamed of fangs and claws and the cold wash of moonlight. You woke up sweating and itching between your legs, your lengthening limbs askew. You thought you should feel horror and revulsion. Instead, you couldn't wait for the wickedness to reveal itself.

It didn't.

Puberty dusted you with new hair, true, but mostly it just betrayed you. You grew tall, but not tall enough. You stayed thin, but not thin enough: your breasts and hips grew until you were shaped like a violin. You hated the way they swayed as you moved. You hated the way they made people look at you, the things they made people say. Someone was always calling you a *beautiful young woman*.

You let your leg, armpit, and pubic hair grow out. You cut the hair on your head short and spiky. It didn't stop the comments. You wanted to die.

Every month, blood spilled from your body. You liked to sniff it furtively in a bathroom stall between classes. Sometimes you wet a finger in the blood. Put the finger in your mouth. The thin bright red tasted different than the clotted dark.

In middle and high school you were still ostracized by your female classmates, but boys started asking you out. You found them boring and unattractive. They were only interested in your body, and in such a timid, tepid way you couldn't even get decent sex out of them. Your first kiss was in seventh grade. Jason F. ran away after you bit his lip hard. You lost your virginity in tenth grade. Steve K. flipped out when he realized you were on your period. You removed your glass eye and threw it at him, and that was the end of that. *Psycho bitch. I'm telling everyone what a psycho bitch you are.*

When you were seventeen, you started going to bars with a fake ID. The ID wasn't that convincing, but you looked a lot older than you were. You drank the bitterest drinks you could find. You made bartenders prepare obscure cocktails you found online, showing them the recipes on your phone. You danced sometimes, when the alcohol was fizzing through you in a numbing joyful wave of forgetfulness.

One night, a man found you dancing. He was the most

handsome man you'd ever seen. Gold stud in one ear. Beard nearly blue. Big eyes, big ears, big teeth. His body wasn't bigger than yours, but it felt bigger. Because he was handsome, and smiling at you, and because you were drunk, you ground against him for half an hour and then let him take you home. He said his name was John when he first introduced himself. He said it was Frank when you were leaving the bar. You let it slide; God, he made you wet.

JohnFrank fucked you hard and everywhere but his bed. He ran a kitchen knife against the inside of your thigh. He tied you at the wrists and ankles with extension cords. He gripped you tight around the throat and squeezed until you saw flowers bloom in your good eye, then disintegrate into burnt-edged holes. He said he was going to kill you, and you could tell from his voice and the shine of his eyes and teeth in the dark that he meant it. You grinned and laughed soundlessly.

His grip relaxed a little.

"God," you croaked. "Don't stop. What are you waiting for?"

His hands left your neck. "What's wrong with you?"

"Nothing," you breathed. "This is the most incredible thing that's ever happened to me. I really want you to do it." Your voice was so scratchy you barely sounded human.

JohnFrank flipped you over and began to untie you. "Well, that takes the fun out of things," he said petulantly.

"Chicken," you said, but the word got lost in a cough.

You looked and waited, in excitement and dread, but you never saw him again.

You left your parents' place at twenty. With your dad's money, you secured a small apartment. You stayed in the city where you'd grown up; it didn't seem worthwhile to move. Everywhere a person like you could go was more or less the same, anyway. You worked retail, then graduated to low-level office jobs. You kept to yourself during the day. At night, you kept going to the bars. Not every night. Maybe three or four times a month. You'd leave around midnight with the best-looking man, or the most violent-looking man, who'd have you. You'd try and convince him to knock you around a little. Some of them kicked you out, or got an Uber home in a hurry. Some of them responded with enthusiasm — beat you, raped you, robbed you.

It wasn't enough. It didn't satisfy. But it was something. You lived for those sparkling, drunken nights of danger. The wickedness inside you stayed trapped, pacing its cage of bone, howling at the moon behind your false eye and your true one. During the day, it slept. And the days were gray and flat and endlessly, frictionlessly boring.

Until you met Tiffany.

She'd been the receptionist at your office for a while. Weeks, maybe months. You didn't notice her until she got into the elevator with you one evening. Instead of ignoring you and avoiding eye contact, she smiled. Asked if you had weekend plans.

"Not really," you said. "Why?"

You didn't bother to keep the hostility out of your voice. Tiffany was your age, about your height and build, but she might as well have belonged to a different species. Her makeup was like something you'd see on a magazine cover; you could barely tell she was wearing it at all. She looked perfect. She wore a slightly old-fashioned skirt suit and matching shoes. There were gold stars in her ears and around her throat. You could smell her laundry detergent, or maybe her perfume, or her soap. Lavender and mint.

"I was just wondering if you wanted to come out with me and the rest of the girls on Saturday night." Her voice was like her scent. Soft, soothing. "You always keep to yourself. I thought you must be lonely."

The rest of the girls. Never in a million years. "I don't think I'm up for a crowd."

"Oh." Small ditch dug between her impeccably groomed eyebrows. "Well, would you like to meet up for a drink tonight, then? Just us? I'm not busy." She seemed so sincere.

You were going to say no. What could someone like Tiffany want with someone like you? The elevator chimed and the door swooshed open. Her smile was lovely.

"Sure," you told Tiffany's pseudo-silk back. "Just tell me where."

You'd been to the Barcade before, but for Tiffany, you pretended you hadn't. The gimmick was all in the name: a bar and a nostalgic arcade, like the kind people ten or twenty years older than you might have haunted as adolescents. There were game machines. Neon lights and tinny, electronic blip-bloops. An incongruous soundtrack of modern pop hits. Carpet like the upholstery covering bus seats. Even a singing animatronic cat lady with big, furry breasts in a black crop top with the Barcade's logo on the front. Tiffany grimaced at her as you walked past on your way to a booth.

"That thing is so gross," she said. "Only part of this place I don't like. I wish they'd get rid of it; not all their customers are college boys."

"I don't mind," you reassured her. "This is all really neat—thanks for showing it to me. What're the best cocktails here?" You slid into red pleather benches, facing each other.

"They do pretty good G and Ts. Usually I just have a couple beers."

You don't like beer, so you ordered a gin and tonic. You ordered four more gin and tonics as you sat and talked and watched the neon rainbows dance across Tiffany's face. Her skin was so smooth. You wanted to touch it. If you were a man, you'd touch it, you thought. If you were a man, you would bring Tiffany home with you and ask her what she wanted you to do and do it all until she was satisfied, until she couldn't stand it anymore, until she came again and again into your mouth and your hands.

The conversation started awkward and slow, but as you both got tipsy it became fluid, funny. Devoid of much meaningful content. You joked about work, let Tiffany share all her office gossip. But you'd have talked about dryer lint to watch Tiffany's mouth move under those shifting lights. She would have made dryer lint seem interesting. Words swam up from her throat like shining bubbles. You laughed, and she looked startled.

"I'm serious, though. Joel from accounting, he's totally bald. I mean, *totally*. No eyebrows, no eyelashes, no anything. It's some kind of disease. He has a really good wig and, like, these fake eyebrows and eyelashes and sideburns he glues on every day. Sheila swears up and down it's true. She even showed me a picture of him where one of the eyebrows was slipping off." She grinned. "It was sort of diving towards his ear, like a little worm."

You laughed again. "That's nothing," you said. You tapped your glass eye. "I'm a cyclops." And you told the whole story of the husky, the accident, the operation you don't remember. With gin fuzzing up your brain, you couldn't tell how Tiffany was taking it. Her face rippled before you. Slick pink lips, eyes the color of a swimming pool. No, a spring leaf. No. Something else.

Suddenly her hand slid over yours. Just for a moment, but it felt like it had burned you, like the imprint of her palm would be branded on your knuckles forever. "I'm so sorry that happened to you," she said. "No wonder you're, well, the way you are. But really, you shouldn't feel insecure about it. Nobody can tell! You look normal. You look pretty."

Your heart swelled; your heart fell. Tiffany didn't understand. But she was trying. She wanted to. You pinched the back of your hand where she'd touched it. Did you want another drink? You couldn't decide.

"It's not about how I look. It's about who I am. It's about what's under my skin."

Tiffany frowned and asked what you meant. She called over a man wearing a tight Barcade t-shirt and ordered another Corona Light. You ordered a Blue Hawaii to mix things up a little. Before it even arrived, you were spilling words across the table. You told her about the man who first choked you, how he was going to kill you.

Tiffany's eyes glistened. She shook her head. Her hand hovered over yours, but did not touch it. "I'm sorry," she said again. "Oh my god, that's incredibly fucked up. I'm so sorry. Listen, there are hotlines you can call if you need to talk to someone about—"

"You still don't understand!" Your interruption was louder than you meant it to be, and you were standing, bristling. You could feel the fur scratching below the surface of your back, trying to break through. People at other tables stared, startled. The waiter arrived with your drinks and you sat back down quickly.

"You don't understand," you said again. "I wanted it. I needed it." You sipped your Blue Hawaii through its long plastic straw, and the night broke apart.

You were laughing and Tiffany was crying. You hugged her and she swayed into you. You were both apologizing for something.

Now you were playing a Beetlejuice-themed pinball game. Losing. The lights and bells shrieked until you couldn't think.

Tiffany stood guard outside the bathroom as you retched into the toilet again and again. There was blood in what came up.

In the parking lot waiting for a ride. Asphalt under you, white-gold stars up above, a grinning moon. You lifted your skirt and pushed aside your underwear and pissed on the ground. The smell was acrid and comforting in its familiarity. Tiffany was making a face at you. Tiffany kept looking at you and then looking at her phone. You kept looking at her and then looking at the moon.

You had your head on her shoulder in the car. A woman was singing about loneliness over a spacy electronic soundscape.

You were at home in your bed and Tiffany wasn't beside you. *Good.* You wanted to have something more special with her. You wanted to be sober the first time. You wanted some sort of tenderness.

~

For the first time you could remember, you spent the rest of the weekend alone in your apartment and happy.

You had forgotten to exchange numbers with Tiffany, so you couldn't text her, but you found her Instagram. You spent hours scrolling through the photos in a shaft of sun. Tiffany with a puppy, with a gaggle of friends, with her mother and grandmother, in a canoe on a lake. Always laughing, starry, summer-eyed.

You didn't have an Instagram account. You thought about making one, just to message her. You kept chickening out, unfolding from your lazy circle on the armchair, pacing the dusty floor, coming back to your phone. There would be time. You'd see her at work soon enough.

When you dreamed, you dreamed she was with you. You gently bit the silky, peach-fuzzed skin around her navel until it mottled and bruised. She flipped you on your back and straddled your chest, her fair hair and pointy, pink-tipped breasts swaying above you. Her hands found your throat and squeezed, and squeezed, until you felt something start to rise. It was coming through your nostrils, your ears, your eye sockets. It was fur, smoke, a sound like the wind at night. You oozed out of your body in the shape of a great black dog, and you took her between your teeth.

In your sleep, your mouth twitched itself into something like a smile.

On Monday, the other receptionist sat behind Tiffany's desk. Lacey or Lindsay or Lily, her name was. She was buck-toothed and dour, with long fake fingernail claws you half-envied.

"Out sick," Lacey-Lindsay-Lily told you, when you asked. *Hungover*, you surmised she meant. You hoped Tiffany would be all right tomorrow. On your lunch break, you bought three blood-red roses in a glass jar.

"Can you make sure Tiffany gets these?" you asked Lacey-Lindsay-Lily.

"Sure." She tapped her claws on the desk. "You wanna leave your name? A card or something?"

You nodded. Asked to borrow some printer paper, scribbled a quick note on it. *Had a great time on Friday! I've never met anyone like you before. Can't wait to see you and talk again! Hope you're feeling better. xoxo*

This morning, Tiffany was back at her usual place. Finally. You'd started to get really worried. Maybe she was sick after all.

When you walked into the office, she beckoned you over. You practically ran.

"I can't accept these." Her voice trembled as she shoved the jar of roses at you. They were wilted. It had been a couple days.

"Why not? It was nothing, I promise. I wanted to give you something."

"I just can't. I'm sorry, it's too weird."

"Do you want to grab lunch together? I've missed you."

"I can't today."

You leaned towards her. She looked pale and tired. "After work, then. Please? We don't have to actually go anywhere. We can just sit on that bench outside the library and catch up for a couple minutes."

She sighed. "Yeah. Okay. Fine." Her voice was stronger now. "That's all right."

Even with the return of the roses, you felt light and full of optimism. You barely ate, barely paid attention to your work, barely noticed the way your co-workers kept giving you sidelong glances and whispering behind their hands. Your blank, bare cube made the roses seem cheerful although their heads had started to crust and curl at the edges. They still smelled alive.

You hummed to yourself as you typed. You were still humming when you left the building. Crossed the road. Walked a block down to the public library where, as promised, Tiffany was waiting on the broad metal bench, picking at its peeling paint. She started, wild-eyed, when you sat down beside her.

"Shit! I didn't see you come up."

"Sorry," you said. "How're you doing? How's your dog? I saw on Instagram he was having tummy problems."

She moved away from you, down the bench. "Don't look at my fucking Instagram!" she snapped. Then, before you had time to react to that unexpected outburst, in a calmer voice: "Listen, don't take this the wrong way, but I don't want to see you again outside of work. I don't think we should be friends. And I'm straight. I don't want to get flowers from other women."

"But I—" Your head whirled. This wasn't anything you'd been expecting. Your feelings tumbled and clashed. It was difficult to form words. "*You're* the one who asked me to go out with you. You're the one who asked in the first place. I thought we had fun." You sounded so plaintive; you hated that.

"I felt sorry for you," said Tiffany. Still calm, condescending, even. "I really did. I was trying to be nice. I thought you were just shy, see, even though everyone else thinks you're weird and stuck up and aloof. Figured I might bring you out of your shell a little."

"And it worked! Look, I swear I didn't mean to make you uncomfortable by coming on to you. We can just be friends. I'm not even really a lesbian, honest. I'll never buy you roses again." You might as well have been on your hands and knees, prostrate.

"That's not the point!" Tiffany snapped again. She must have hated your whining and begging as much as you did. "It worked, but you know— some people ought to stay inside their shells! I can't handle being friends with you!"

"What do you mean? Tell me what you mean!" You moved towards her on the bench, pushing her back until she was cornered against one of its curlicue armrests. You could smell her toothpaste. You could see a glimmer of fear in her face, and you liked it.

She shoved you aside and sprang to her feet. Her hands were fists, her cheeks flushed. "I mean that you're a freak. You're a fucking nutcase! You need professional help! You're a drunk and you're sexually confused and you have these absolutely demented fantasies and you don't know how to tell when you're making other people feel scared and uncomfortable! Or maybe you just don't *care!*"

It certainly wasn't the first time you'd heard any of this. For some reason, though, it all felt new. Each truth was a glass knife plunged between your ribs and pulled downward, razing your heart and your breath and your very bones. You were coming apart. You were dying. You wanted to be dead. You wanted to have never existed at all. The thing that hid inside you uncoiled itself. It pressed hard against the back of your skin— more knives, or pins and needles, each one forcing itself through a pore.

You fell forward onto the sidewalk, scraping your palms. There was a pressure building in your skull. Blood began to drip slowly from your nose and mouth. It seemed too bright.

Tiffany was saying your name. She sounded concerned. It might have been enough, but she was still backing away, moving farther from you, her hands hovering in front of her chest. A defensive posture, protecting her vital organs.

You erupted from your old body, skin and clothes shredding across new muscle and wet pelt. Your glass eye popped from your face like a cork from a bottle, and you realized you could see depth again. Two eyes, new eyes. Only, the colors were different.

You stood on all fours, your tail alert, your ears full of sounds and your snout full of scent. Hunger prodded you to give chase as Tiffany screamed and began to run, heels clacking, hair flying. It was easier to get the hang of your new shape than you would have thought, but you were not thinking now. *You are not thinking.* Only moving in pursuit, moving on instinct, finally unfettered.

YOU BITE TIFFANY'S NECK. You hold her down with your massive paws while you bite out her right eye and swallow it like a piece of candy. There are gunshots. Some commotion. It doesn't matter. Still alive, Tiffany sobs underneath you. She's trying to say something with her smeared red mouth. That doesn't matter, either.

Behind you, beside the shabby library bench, the remains of what you were ripple in the breeze like ribbons in a little girl's hair.

MACRAMÉ FLAMES

ERIC RAGLIN

*H*ow Thorpe went from being a member of the Nightmare Queers motorcycle gang to a suburbanite with a respectable carpentry business is beyond me.

Back when we were committing arson once or twice a week, he always threw the first Molotov, and boy did his eagerness for destruction win my heart. After one arson in Cincinnati, we fled the scene, climbed to a nearby rooftop, and went to town on each other while the Hobby Lobby below burned—one of six Hobby Lobbies we'd torched that month alone. Watching the cops scramble to find us and fail only furthered our pleasure.

"They're dumb as shit," Thorpe groaned, his Gimli beard buried in my ass. "Thank Satan for that."

After a couple of sweaty, sexy hours, we fell asleep on the rooftop. Reckless, I know, but waking up to a sunrise hazy with craft supply smoke was magical. Shivering in our leather jackets, we held each other and shared a cigarette. Perfect beauty and calm enveloped us. I would've loved for the moment to last forever, but you rarely get to savor things when you're wanted in seventeen states.

Before the morning rush hour, we were off to the next Hobby Lobby. Not another in Ohio—we weren't stupid—but one a few hundred miles off, the stores growing fewer and farther between. Gang leader Ripley greeted our arrival with eyes narrowed and tattooed arms crossed. She gave us shit for spending the night so close to the crime scene, but I didn't care. And from the way she smirked, it seemed neither did she. It was impossible to resent such a goddamn cute couple.

Still, there were limits to our love. When the gang broke up five years back, I refused to settle in the suburbs with Thorpe among the golfers, HOA shitheads, and Quiverfull families next door. Loaded with cash from years of robberies and inexplicably good financial planning, Thorpe sought stability after his homeless teenage years and his on-the-run twenties. My wanderlust hadn't yet been satisfied, though. I left to bike around the country alone, doing odd jobs and keeping a low profile, but it wasn't the same without him. Even in the company of other men—at truck stops and campsites, in bathhouses and porta potties—I thought of Thorpe constantly. I often flipped through pictures I'd taken on the road and imagined he was in them: standing among Yellowstone bison with casual fearlessness, slamming back rotgut shots in a San Francisco gay bar, and gazing at the stars through a tent's mesh roof. The two of us together, inseparable.

It was only after the gang realized our Satanic work wasn't done that I saw him again. Like a heist movie, he came out of retirement for one last job. Maybe because he remembered what made us so good together, or maybe because suburbia bored him. Guess I'll never know. I missed my chance to ask.

~

RIPLEY'S PROPHECY promised literal Hell on Earth after we burned down 666 Hobby Lobbies, but somehow we fucked up the count. It's true what they say about queers and math. Ripley's partner Xena miscounted, so we thought our work was done, which meant Hell didn't come to Earth, causing Ripley's prophecy to lose credibility and the gang to split up. Kinda funny in retrospect. I stayed gang-loyal longer than Thorpe and most of the others, but at some point it got awkward. It was only Ripley and Xena, plus me third-wheeling it, and you know how a biker feels about anything with more than two wheels. I bounced.

Thing is, Xena did an arson recount five years later. Why, you're wondering? For her goddamn scrapbook. Every Hobby Lobby arson news clipping got its own page, and when she glued the final article to page 665, she must have thought, *Huh, I done fucked up.* Sure did, Warrior Princess.

After that, Ripley informed the gang of the situation through an encrypted group text, though there were fewer of us now: Nox had died in a knife fight with some Sturgis Nazis, Kip had died in a knife fight with herself, and Dozer had fucked off to DJ at a queer nightclub in Berlin. Those who remained—minus a stubbornly silent Thorpe—hopped on a video conference call like real corporate ghouls, but instead of suits and ties, we each had face tats and septum piercings and crooked scheming smiles. We shot the shit and plotted for hours. I left the call fucking buzzing, thinking if everything went smoothly, Hell really would come to Earth. It'd be a 24/7 paradise for queers and anarchists and the best sorts of criminals.

Hobby Lobby still hadn't recovered from the Nightmare Queers' campaign of terror, but they'd dared to open one new location in Omaha, Nebraska. The corporation had waited a good three years after our spree ended to build it, and there it had stood ever since with the store sign glowing orange like a beacon for crafty evangelist assholes. Ripley and Xena scouted the place ahead of time. There was a security camera at the store's southeast corner and a blindspot on the northwest side of the parking lot. We'd taken on much harder jobs, so this one should've been cake, right?

The morning before our final arson, after too many unreturned voicemails, I drove to Thorpe's suburban hellscape to plead my case. His lawn was perfect, and by perfect, I mean perfectly fucking boring: mowed and watered and monoculture as all hell. A wooden welcome sign hung from the door. It looked like one you'd find at Hobby Lobby, but as I found out later that day, he'd made it himself. Arsonist, ass-eater, and carpenter—Thorpe was a triple threat.

When I knocked, he answered with a shaved face and his shirt tucked into his pants. The shirt thing threw me off. What kind of person tucked their shirt in while lazing around at home? Didn't seem like the Thorpe I'd known. Still, he was willing to hear me out on this one last job, and I was willing to open my heart again, carefully, like opening a door during a hailstorm.

"How would you feel about fucking up one last craft store?" I asked, going in for a kiss.

Thorpe lurched back and whispered, "Not so loud. Come in.'"

Whether he was afraid of getting busted for criminal activity or getting outed as a homo in Trump country, I couldn't tell, but I followed him inside. He shut the door, then gave me a quick peck on the corner of my mouth. A totally unromantic reunion kiss, but it had also been five-fucking-years of radio silence, so who could blame him?

Thorpe had a black pleather sectional couch without a single cracked cushion, a big-ass TV covering half the wall, and a spinning rack of home improvement magazines.

"Nice house," I said through a grimace. "Please say you've got an altar room somewhere. A little Satan in the suburbs."

"I don't worship much of anything these days," Thorpe

said, scratching his shaved neck. Not even a shadow of stubble remained.

"Maybe that'll change tonight," I said. "We've got the count right this time, so big things could happen."

Thorpe nodded and gave a polite Midwestern smile, but didn't make eye contact. Silence took hold, filled by the soft hum of air conditioning. Not even a window unit—this was bougie-ass central cooling.

"Listen, I know this is awkward and you don't really want to deal with gang shit anymore, but..." I cleared my throat, "do you at least wanna have sex? For old time's sake."

"Sure," he said. "That would be nice."

A GOOD CUM broke the ice. Thorpe and I laid in his Tempur-Pedic bed (could've gotten used to that bed, holy shit), cuddling naked and drinking whiskey and catching up on half a decade of lost love. He braided my hair just like he used to, which made me cry a few boozy tears. When I stopped crying, it was his turn.

"I hate myself most of the time," he sniffled. "I needed safety and security, and...and I sold out for it. This life—it's comfortable and it's nice and it's so goddamn boring. The neighborhood dads invited me to join an Eagles cover band. The Eagles, for Satan's sake!"

"Satan, you say?"

He smiled, then kissed me. It was wet and tonguey and way fucking hotter than our kiss at the door.

Pulling away abruptly, he asked, "Do you hate me?"

I almost laughed at the audacity of that question.

"Thorpe, you have to understand," I said, "two years back, I biked through this town that had a custom body pillow shop—no lie—and I seriously fucking considered getting one printed with a picture of you. I was pathetic and lonely and totally head over heels for this bitch right in front of me. So, no, I could never hate you."

Thorpe's smile lasted only a moment before he sobbed into my armpit and whispered "thank you, I love you" over and over and over. I cradled his head and inhaled him. He was already starting to smell more like the man I remembered. Maybe there'd be a future for us after all. I wondered if I could persuade him to burn down this house (but not the bed!) and collect the insurance money. We'd ride off together and enjoy a lifelong road trip through Hell on Earth. But I was getting ahead of myself. I'd wait to ask until after the Hobby Lobby burned.

THORPE and I pulled into Omaha late, just like old times. He hadn't ridden his Kawasaki in ages, so we had to do some last-minute maintenance. I felt like a dad yelling at his son to hurry up and get dressed for church, your mom's already in the goddamn car. Still, with a little extra speed on the interstate (and boy, did that feel good), we arrived just ten minutes past midnight. Seven other Nightmare Queers were already there, quietly chatting and smoking under an awning. They waved at us and whisper-shouted an enthusiastic greeting. Standing a ways off, Ripley glared when we pulled into the dark corner of the parking lot, but she grinned at the sight of Thorpe's shaved face.

"I've seen twinks become bears, but never the other way around," she said, hugging him tight. "Good to have you back."

"Glad to be back," Thorpe said, but his voice trembled. Maybe he'd been a suburbanite for so long that returning to crime scared him, light years distant as he was from his roots and values.

I nudged his ribs and whispered, "It's going to be great."

He gave a brief, lippy smile. Before I could give further reassurance, Ripley pushed a Molotov into my hands.

"Still got a good throwing arm?" she asked.

"Hard to miss a fifty-thousand square foot building," I said.

Thorpe snorted and looked down. He kicked over someone's discarded Monster energy can and watched its remnants pool at his feet. Ripley approached him with a second Molotov.

"You spilled my drink," she said.

Thorpe's head snapped up and his eyes went wide.

"Fucking with you, man. I don't drink that shit," Ripley said. She rested a hand on Thorpe's leather jacket, which he probably hadn't worn in years. "You okay?"

Thorpe nodded. "Yeah. I really missed everyone. Things haven't been easy and I...I'm sorry I haven't been around. I really should've—"

"No reason to apologize. The past is the past, and the future is Hell on Earth. Let's torch this craft store and grab a fucking beer."

Thorpe puffed his cheeks out, then hopped up and down like an antsy gay football player on the sidelines. Ripley's pep talk reminded me of why we'd followed her for so many years, and I was grateful she could inspire Thorpe in ways I couldn't.

Ripley called to the others: "Finish your smokes and come here. Don't want cops arriving before we get this party started."

Everyone walked over, hugged me and Thorpe, and then huddled around Ripley. The gang looked different after five years away: Xena had gray hair, Merk had "DADDY" knuckle tats, and Corsica had a half-sagging face from her stroke. Despite the changes, it still felt like old times. I couldn't stop smiling.

"After the building burns, the ground will start shaking.

Don't panic," Ripley said. "That's supposed to happen. It means He's coming."

"Hail Satan," Xena said.

Everyone repeated after her, even Thorpe. I grinned as if I were witnessing his Satanic confirmation. Thorpe could still get right with the Dark Lord.

Ripley pushed a Molotov into Thorpe's hands.

"Will you do the honors," she said, but it wasn't really a question. Thorpe throwing first was all part of the ritual. He was our good luck charm, the reason the cops never caught us. At least that's what Ripley told us.

Thorpe nodded, half-smiled, and then blushed. He cleared his throat.

"Does someone have a lighter?" he asked. "I know I should have brought one, but I quit smoking and—"

"Oh, good for you, man," Ripley said, then handed him a Bic that looked like it'd been a dog's chew toy.

Blinking quickly, Thorpe mumbled a "thank you" before lighting the cloth.

That's when the red and blue lights of two cop cars lit up the parking lot like a fascist disco. Thorpe jumped at the siren's WHOOP and dropped the lit Molotov. It shattered at his feet, and flames consumed him head to toe. I smelled the musk of burning leather, the sharpness of melting hair. Thorpe's high-pitched scream pierced the night. Everyone else's screams followed.

"Shit! Roll, Thorpe, roll!" I said. It felt ridiculous coming out of my mouth, but what else was there to say?

A cop barked through a crackling megaphone: "All of you, hands where I can see them!"

More flame than man, Thorpe made a shrieking sprint toward the Hobby Lobby and dove head-first through the glass door. The pane shattered, and there he lay motionless. Somewhere behind me, Ripley whipped out her gun and fired at the cops. I was frozen with horror, knowing Thorpe and I would never bike a desert highway, get piss-drunk and whisper sweet everythings under the blanket of glittering constellations. We'd never raise a toast to the King of Hell, never party with winged imps in black latex suits, never see the fruits of our Satanic labors.

More shots, and not the celebratory kind. I was out in the fucking open, the rest of the gang ducking behind their bikes and pulling out their pieces. I could only tilt my head toward Thorpe, lifeless and flaming in the Hobby Lobby entrance, his body the accelerant in one final, beautiful act of arson. But something was different about this fire. It spread through the store impossibly fast, Thorpe's accidental sacrifice channeling Satanic magic and feeding the flame's hunger. Firefighters would never put this one out.

A dozen deafening shots. Bullets pinged off of the cop cars and bikes. A cop yelled at me to get the fuck down, then pulled the trigger not a second later. I was lucky he had shit aim because I was still paralyzed watching Thorpe turn to ash fifty feet away.

Another cruiser pulled into the lot with lights spinning. Ripley screamed "fuck, fuck, fuck" and emptied the rest of her clip toward the backup. But the red and blue lights paled in comparison to the Hobby Lobby, shining bright as the Morning Star. A bullet clipped my ear, and I only realized it when hot blood tickled my cheek. Everything was ringing. More shots, then a gut-wrenching scream from Ripley. I couldn't see her, but I knew she'd been hit. Xena shouted to Ripley, her panic-shredded voice repeatedly promising everything would be okay.

And then the earth shook with ecstatic violence. All gunfire stopped. I fell to the ground, which would've made that fucking cop happy had he not been worried about the cracking concrete beneath him. Now he and his boys were screaming and Ripley was laughing and I was crying and Thorpe was burning and dying and rebirthing the world.

Flames spouted, not from the Hobby Lobby, but from the splitting concrete. A screaming cop straddled the scorching crack, but the gap widened and the flames licked the hair off his balls. He fell into the engines of Hell, fuel for Satan's chariot. His car followed, then another car, pulling the second cop down with its open driver's side door. When the last cop tried running—bless his cold, wife-beating heart—a blackened claw thick as a redwood reached up from the quaking crack and gripped his ankle. One tug and he was gone, soul not claimed but rather immolated out of existence. Hell didn't want him, I'm sure of that.

When the claw extended back into the burning night, it stretched endlessly, towering over the Hobby Lobby, the city, the world. Glowing magma hissed through its veins and shards of volcanic glass fell from its fingers, clinking to the ground.

Ever the dumbass, I didn't register what the beast was at first, but I'd just lost my lover and my one good ear, so cut me some fucking slack. Ripley, on the other hand, giggled and rejoiced through labored breath: "Hail Satan, come at last!"

My attention strayed to the Hobby Lobby entrance where not even one of Thorpe's briny balls remained. At least his death meant something. I sobbed and screamed and thanked him and praised Satan and yearned to fill the emptiness inside me. I'd never get to know this reborn world with the man I loved, the man who'd made it possible.

Concrete splintered as the colossal beast's head surfaced, leaving half the parking lot a sinkhole to Hell. Smoke rising from its horns, it turned toward me. That's when I realized I'd given up hope too soon. Meeting my gaze from a mile above, the beast grinned with stalactite fangs hanging over a Gimli beard—the beard I'd longed to feel against my face for so long. A great warmth filled me.

Love and Hell would reign together for eternity.

HELIOGABALUS FABULOUS

BELLE TOLLS

A rain of roses. Erections. The boy king, drops of sweat forming on his almost-mustachioed upper lip, is surveying the courtyard when *she* calls.

Grandmother.

"Marcus!"

Imperious, matronly, she glides into view, her voice still echoing off the palace stone. She blankly regards the scene playing out in the courtyard—nakedness!—youth!—lust!—flowers! Elagabalus, the one she calls Marcus, has created this divine spectacle by releasing flowers from a false ceiling. Tanned bodies curtained by petals. Music plays. She looks over the mess of flowers and bodies at him.

"Marcus."

We hate her hair like that. Pushed up at the front like Neptune's shield, a tidal wave of iron.

"Dear grandmother," he answers. Marcus? Elagabalus! Named in honor of the great god of the mountain, El-Gabal, the unconquered sun god. Ave!

"This is a marvelous spectacle, Marcus," she says, gesturing to the field of roses, narcissi, oleanders, violets, lilies, irises, poppies, amaranths and wildflowers that Elaga-balus has just showered over his guests. "But you are needed at the Senate."

Boy king pulls the tiara from his head. My heart breaks.

I (the one telling you this story) am the third figure from the right in the lower part of the painting by Sir Lawrence Alma Tadema, *The Roses of Heliogabalus* (1888). Note that I am the one the emperor regards. I might seem unimpressed at the flowers, but that's not it at all; of all the goddesses, Flora is the dearest to me. The garlands the emperor and I make to crown each other in our bed are little sacrifices to Her. I'm just tired of the advances from the person to my right. Livia? Take a hint.

No one died in the rain of roses. Another lie of the historians.

Elagabalus, or Marcus, walks between the columns toward his grandmother, and they disappear into the cool shade of the palace. A warm wind blows, the flowers stir and scent the air. I turn over on my couch and think of his cock, circumcised now. In my mind, I suck him off on the imperial throne. Into the back of my throat. The sweat from his balls reaches my lip. The sweat on his lip again. I pull his thighs up, sliding his ass forward, licking the hair at his hole. The solar anus of the Sun King. My bride.

I stand up from my couch and go to our chamber to wait for the business of government to be over with.

Nearby, in the sanctum on Palatine Hill, the black mete-orite, El-Gabal, throbs with primeval energy. Time, libido, concentration all warp and seem to pulse when you stand too close. The old priests sense it and move away uneasily.

∾

IN OUR ROOM THAT NIGHT, Elagabalus is beating his face with white powders inherited from his former wives. The burnished mirror casts an eerie bronze light. He adds the blood of berries to his lips, making them a violent purple. It makes his kisses bitter, but that pleases me.

"Will you go out tonight?" I ask.

"Yes, Hierocles." He sounds far away. In his mind he is already with other lovers. Sailors. Ex-slaves. Butchers' boys. Hairy, hard hands pull at his mouth and his dress. I turn over.

"What did you talk about at the Senate today?"

"Severus Alexander."

"Your cousin?"

"Yes." He adds color to his cheeks. "He's fifteen now. Grandmother would like to involve him in the administration."

"As what?"

"As caesar." A title I should have had, except Grandmother objected. "And what will you do this evening, my husband?" Elagabalus is bored with talk of state. Or worried?

"Drink with your mother. Wonder where you are."

I know where he, who calls himself my mistress, will be, more or less, because on nights like tonight he often feels himself called into the city streets, the hot nights in the lower parts of Rome, disguised among the people. To receive them. Taking his citizens inside of himself. Coming home with a full purse—the sacredness of his being fucked consecrated further by receiving coin. Sex work is work. The work of the gods. Divine service. We kiss good night.

JULIA SOAEMIAS BASSIANA, ELAGABALUS' mother, is a second mother to me. Though she is noble and rich and I am a former slave, child of a slave, and maybe the reason why the Guards murmur about our emperor, I feel she loves me. She loves me because he loves me. Her heart is like a great hearth for him, always glowing with welcome.

"I like to drink with you because you're such easy company, Hierocles."

I laugh softly. We have been speaking about her family and I've been listening quietly. Receiving an education in religion.

"El-Gabal's blessings are well known everywhere. In Carthage, a great center of His worship, they grew rich through the sacrifices they offered the great god, who they called Ba'al Hammon—the brazier!—Were you the firstborn in your family, Hierocles?"

"Yes."

"You would have gone into the fiery pit." She laughs. Grim staccato. "We have brought him to Rome, and every barbaric tribe that falls to Rome will also fall to El-Gabal! This is the beginning of a great ascent." Her eyes flicker with the fire-light, and I see furnaces.

As I walk back to our rooms later that night, I think of my home in Caria, of Gordius, who taught me how to steer char-iots and fuck, of my love for Elagabalus, all only alternatives to the cult of Ba'al, the burning babies, me burning.

He wakes me up screaming about his sex again. Terror-ized by his own body. Shaking. Crying so hard he seems to stop breathing at moments. I hold him. Her. My queen, still powdered, dress falling from her shoulders.

When the historian Dio called Elagabalus by feminine pronouns, was he mocking her or honoring her true nature?

SINCE ELAGABALUS TOOK power through the machinations of Grandmother, Rome has become a very different place. It only took a few years. Women come to the senate now. Jupiter has been supplanted as the king of the gods by a foreigner, El-Gabal, the god for whom my love is high priest. Not everyone is happy that the pantheon has a new daddy.

Coming from Emesa to reclaim the seat of power, with Grandmother in the fore like a ship's prow, this clan brought with them a strange black stone sent from heaven, and placed it at the heart of a new temple to which all the holy trinkets of the other gods were brought, so that no god may be honored beyond the presence of this inky thing from the night sky. Grandmother seems indifferent to spiritual questions, but the young king and his mother are devout. Zealous, even.

The god embodied in stone is at the center of our thoughts this morning, as the sun rises over the palace walls and my love wakes, tired of tears but still yearning to be delivered from his sex; imagining a holy operation, the physician's knife, a blessing from Asclepius, to be cut and healed, to open herself for the sun god, a dawning of new light in the world. Sol Invictus.

What does it mean to be called into light-bearing in this way? I contemplate this as she wakes more fully and looks at me.

"I love you," I say. She knows.

"We have to kill Alexander."

THREE QUIET DAYS pass before all of Roman society is ordered to the Hill for a feast in honor of our strange new god. El-Gabal has been brought out into the daylight, glinting black in the hot sun and regarded warily by the nearby Guards.

Tables overflow with food and wine is dispensed to everyone present. The censers burn with strange drugs. The emperor arrives in high drag. Her beauty is sickening, radiant. There are no speeches – drumming starts immediately.

Among the matrons, Julia Soaemias Bassiana alone is ecstatic, rapturously watching her child begin the divine rite. Grandmother scans the gathering surreptitiously, clearly anxious that this cultic display will further upset the patrician class to whom she owes her current power.

In time with the drums, Elagabalus begins to move, first from side to side and soon in short steps around the great god. The meteorite glints and seems to sweat. The crowd, some drunk but all beginning to feel the effects of the votive smoke, look fixedly at the sight of their kingly queen. Elagabalus dances around the stone. The drumming becomes more rapid, as does the dance. She is strutting. Dipping and swaying. Slipping free from her dress, pulling it after her like a great banner, her naked body is adorned with sigils; Are they glowing with black light?

The crowd is spellbound, moving to the music. Closest to the censers, the vestal virgins vomit. Jupiter's priest watches at a distance, his face fixed in a hateful grimace. But El-Gabal is fully present now. The stone surges with black light. Ave! Ave! Ave!

Through the smoke and stygian glow, visions materialize and dissipate. Androgyne angels, science and theory unfetter us, kings become queens, and queens kings. Children grow free as flowers. There are senates of women, senates without sex, all the statues fall—gods and generals alike—everyone is crowned in flowers, the works of Sappho are known everywhere. Beauty reigns!

Elagabalus is dancing a future into existence before the people of Rome, who clamor with delight at the spectacles of liberation emanating out of the stone's black fire.

And now I strike. We don't want to wait for that distant future, beyond dark ages, beyond inquisitions, beyond laws and executions and beatings to death. Queer intifada now!

I seize Alexander and pull him with me toward the stone. A sacrifice. Let the young patriarch burn for the future to come. He struggles weakly, and I overpower him, dragging him forward into the queer mist.

But my adrenaline blinds me to the actions of Grandmother, ever decisive, never losing sight of the political circumstances. She has not allowed herself to succumb to the smoke and calls in the Guard. The crowd erupts. A table is overturned, people shout, someone is trampled. The god makes a sickening noise, throbbing as the images fade.

In the tumult, I lose my love. They have danced into exhaustion, into their mother's arms, and both are quickly arrested by the Guards. It is all over as soon as it's begun. No liberation. Not now. The executions are summary and immediate – they have been approved in advance by Grandmother. She knew well before we did how the tide was turning against us, how the citizens complained of extravagances, tableaux for Flora, nightly escapades by the bordellos, how the Praetorian Guard (all closeted tops) made a show of their disgust for the effeminacies they saw permeating the capital. In an instant, Jupiter is back in fashion.

Here comes the death blow.

BEHEADED and dragged through the city, Julia's body is discarded to be eaten by stray dogs. Elagabalus' is thrown in the Tiber. To the grunting guards they were a headless body, crashing through rapids, against rocks and, later, gently bobbing among the reeds. Deposed faggot. Dead at eighteen. Headless but haloed, divine prostitute, sexless monarch forced to play king, finally supplanted by more forgettable kings.

Grandmother remains the puppeteer throughout Severus Alexander's reign and the meteorite is sent back to Emesa. The Guards come for me too; no more festivals of flowers.

Who needs a body anyway? Like I'm not in the furnace of

Ba'al, I know my love is not lying among the brushes: They are streaming in perfect light to the future. No more Jupiter, no more Senate, no more caesars. Lilacs instead; flowers everywhere! Genderfuck; divinity! They danced a world into being that can't be un-danced, and it's approaching us like light, light, light, light!

ACKNOWLEDGMENTS

MAE MURRAY

This book would not have been possible without the faith and support of so many folks, it's overwhelming to sit down and take stock of them all. As I write this, I have tears in my eyes and my heart is aflame with gratitude for:

All the Kickstarter backers, including those who donated in the top-tier category: Annie Oddly, Caleb Rogers, Geoffrey Keel, Rebecca A. Burrows, Tasheina Skywalker, Noble Brennan, Miss Quinn Swain-Nisbet, and Noelle Burley—who has been my close friend for almost two decades and has all my love.

To Sam Richard and Eric Raglin, who pooled their extensive publishing knowledge and graciously shared it with me. This book, quite literally, would not exist had you not shared my passion for the idea. To Eric LaRocca, Hailey Piper, and Joe Koch for inspiring me, for being essential voices in the queer horror community, for changing the landscape and challenging everything with your fresh ideas and prose.

To everyone who submitted, hyped, rallied behind me when I was tired and full of doubt.

To the artists who contributed Kickstarter materials: Arran and Jay of Pearl Street Tattoo Club, Marko Head, and Kelly Thomas.

And finally to my family: My partner Jim for enduring my tears and holding me tight these past 7 years, my Grandma Judy—the OG horror fan of my life, my best friend, my greatest love—and to Dad, who would have hated this book but would have been proud I made it anyway.

Medusa Publishing Haus is a micro press dedicated to uplifting new and unique voices in the horror genre.

Updates on past and current releases can be found at www.medusahaus.com.